Diameter of the Bullet

Tammy Kaiser

with

Mia Kaiser

INTRODUCTION

This book uses the actual experiences of the authors to inform the fictional characters in the story. This book was born of blood and pain, hope and recovery.

The quotes at the beginning of each entry were added by the authors to illustrate the vast knowledge of humanity and to underscore the importance of sharing our stories.

This book is also a tool. There is a glossary of words, as well as questions for thought and discussion in the back of this book. Think, reflect, learn, and always share your own story.

"I decided to devote my life to telling the story because I felt that having survived I owe something to the dead. And anyone who does not remember betrays them again."

Elie Wiesel

DIAMETER OF THE BULLET

AFTERMATH

RUBY

"There would always be before, during, and after. And nothing would ever bridge the three."

Elise Blackwell, *Hunger*

My mom almost died. That's why I have to write this journal. Dr. Sanderson says it will help me sort through my feelings. "Sometimes," she says, "putting things in order helps our mind make sense out of the senseless." I'm not sure what that means. All I know is, I have to come up with a topic for each letter of the alphabet related to my mom almost dying and what it's been like since then. And, I am not allowed to skip around. I need to go from A to Z. I need to put things in order. Seems a bit rigid to me but Dr. Sanderson used to work in a hospital Trauma Intensive Care Unit and she knows how to help people "navigate trauma". She also worked at Hospice getting people ready to die. Creepy. Dr. Sanderson says this journal is supposed to be private so I can express myself freely but she hopes I'll find some things to discuss with her while writing. So, 'A' stands for Alphabetical Journal. And, Aftermath – that was Dr. Sanderson's idea.

Aftermath means the consequences or aftereffects of an event. In my case, the event was a shooting at my mom's work, a Jewish charity, and the

3

consequences are probably the fact that I am seeing a therapist a year later because things still aren't back to normal – whatever that is.

Mom found Dr. Sanderson through Jewish Family Services. Dr. Sanderson isn't Jewish but Mom and I are. Plus, she takes our insurance. My mom and I haven't been getting along well lately. I want her to stop worrying so much and she wants me to "understand". Apparently, Dr. Sanderson is going to help me "understand" and another doctor is going to help Mom stop worrying. Or something like that.

I have to see Dr. Sanderson twice a month. Dr. Sanderson told me she won't read my journal unless I want her to. Mom said that I should allow Dr. Sanderson to read everything. She said that the doctor can't help me unless I let her. She also said that if I listen to Dr. Sanderson and follow directions, she'll buy me a $50 gift card. That's cool, I guess.

So, here I am on my bed as the rain slips down the window and pools on the sill because the seal is broken, writing in a red spiral notebook with my appointment time on the front. Tuesdays, 4 pm. There's a yellow sticky note with my second appointment date stuck to the cover: July 28th. What a fun way to spend the rest of my summer, in a shrink's office. I guess it's better than last summer. Anything is better than last summer.

* * *

Dr. Sanderson is nice, I guess. She has a daughter, Hailey, who's also 14 and Dr. Sanderson likes to make comparisons. My hair is brown like my mom's. Hailey's is the same shade of blonde as Dr. Sanderson's. I like pop music. Hailey likes Jazz. I had my Bat Mitzvah when I was thirteen. Hailey won her first track meet, or whatever they call it, when she was twelve. I think Dr. Sanderson talks about her daughter to make me feel comfortable, like she knows me because she has a kid my age and that makes her an automatic expert or something. It's kind of annoying, but she seems like a nice mom. She let Hailey get her nose pierced for her thirteenth birthday which my mom would never do. My mom has to process everything first. She has to weigh the pros and cons and research possible outcomes and solutions. It takes her forever to make a decision. That's probably why it took her so long to get me therapy after the shooting. I bet Dr. Sanderson would have gotten Hailey therapy right away.

Dr. Sanderson says we have to work on recreating the pathways in my brain. A year of pathways have been formed informing my thoughts and feelings and I am supposed to reroute my brain somehow. She keeps telling me I need to draw a new roadmap. Apparently I am a trauma survivor. The trauma she's talking about is the shooting. But it's not just the shooting. It's the way Mom has changed since the shooting. She's different. So am I. We used to laugh a lot. She used to be my best friend. Now, she's just sort of...there. Not really much of anything. It's like she just wants to get through a day without something bad happening. Then she takes a pill to help her sleep. That's pretty much life right now. Dr. Sanderson says I need to reflect on what is different about me since the shooting. What things did I do before that I don't do now? What interests did I have before the shooting? Are they different now? I never really thought about how I've changed. I can see so many changes in my mom, but not in myself. I guess I did laugh at jokes and hang out with my friends more. I cared more about their lives. I don't care as much about the boys they like or the clothes they buy. It seems silly now. Like, that stuff doesn't really matter.

ADRENALINE

NAOMI

"Do one thing that scares you every day."

Eleanor Roosevelt

Why am I doing this? Because Ruby is doing it, and Ruby means everything to me.

It has been one year since the shooting.

This is the hardest thing I've ever done. Surviving.

Ruby was given an alphabetical journal assignment by her new therapist. She started yesterday. The assignment: to write a journal entry for every letter of the alphabet A to Z. No skipping letters. Ruby told me her first entry is titled Aftermath. She won't let me read her journal. I understand. They are her thoughts and her feelings. Dr. Willer will help me work through my thoughts and feelings while Dr. Sanderson helps Ruby.

I didn't really know what my first entry should be. I was thinking Aftermath. It is a really good beginning. Beginning with the end, sort of. But, I don't want to steal a page from Ruby's book. So, I decided on Adrenaline.

There is this thing called an adrenaline rush. People try to get a rush of the hormone adrenaline on purpose because they like the way it feels. There are even articles about how to induce such a "rush". Watch a scary movie. Ride a roller coaster. Visit a haunted house.

Or, I guess, be in a shooting.

When human senses perceive a stress such as danger or a threat, cells in the nervous and endocrine systems work together to prepare the body for action. I read that in an article. Most people refer to this as the "fight or flight" response. We fight or we run away.

The respiratory rate increases. Blood is directed into the muscles and limbs, which require extra energy and fuel for running and fighting. The pupils dilate. Awareness intensifies. Sight sharpens. Impulses quicken. I read that in an article too.

I read a lot of articles. I want to understand my body. Especially since I don't feel I have much control over it anymore.

We fight. Or we run away. Or we hide.

* * *

I waited a year to get us into therapy. I was selfish. I was thinking of what *I* needed, and not what Ruby needed. I should have gotten both of us help much earlier. I was so busy trying to keep myself together that I risked letting Ruby fall apart.

Ruby is my everything.

Aftermath – after the shooting. I love that she used that word to begin her journal.

Sometimes, I only remember the after. Was there ever a before?

BULLETS

RUBY

"It's very dramatic when two people come together to work something out. It's easy to take a gun and annihilate your opposition, but what is really exciting to me is to see people with differing views come together and finally respect each other."

Fred Rogers

The average speed for a 9mm handgun bullet is about 1100 feet per second. The diameter of the bullet is roughly 9.01mm. That was the gun "the gunman" used. I have to call him the gunman because I don't want to use his real name. He has one. His parents named him a real name and loved him when he was a baby and a little boy. They probably packed his lunch and watched him play violin in his school concerts. They may have supervised play dates and chaperoned real dates. They probably watched *Sesame Street* together and ate macaroni and cheese or corn-dogs. I wonder if the gunman's parents ever taught him to hate Jews and to one day grow up to shoot them. Did he attend a Jew-hating preschool?

In all the media interviews after the attack his parents seemed so sad, so shocked and remorseful. Like, they could never imagine their son doing such a thing. But he was on the security camera. They didn't have to imagine anything. After the trial, the video overwhelmed the media. I

9

watched the bullets meant for my mom over and over on the 6 o'clock news.

She was sitting at her desk when he came in. She had kicked off her shoes and was responding to an email. That's when she heard what she thought were balloons popping. Then screaming.

Mom couldn't even go to the fall fair because the people screaming on the roller coaster would make her cry and not be able to breathe. She said the screaming on the day the gunman came was the worst screaming she had ever heard in her life. And the sound of the bullets hitting things – walls, people – everything was amplified. Mom hid under her desk. She crouched as low as she could and listened for footsteps. She snuck out once and locked her office door. She was shaking. Mom says her whole world became *that* moment, in that office. Her desk, the carpet, the file cabinet that held client files, the old-fashioned crank window.

Mom can't really run faster than 1100 feet per second. But, she can jump.

And she did – right out the window.

At first I was mad at my mom. Why didn't she leave her office and fight? Why didn't she call 911? Why didn't she try to save people? All she did was run away and she hurt her back and legs in the process. The gunman may not have shot her, but she was still injured. Dr. Sanderson says that it is normal to feel angry. She says I can feel anger toward my mom, the gunman, people who got out, people who died. I've only ever really been angry with Mom. I'm not as angry as I used to be. I understand that Mom wasn't really thinking. She just reacted. I know that Mom couldn't have really fought a man with a gun. I get it. But my mom was my hero. Up until she became a victim. Now, she's just a mom. A mom who waited a year to get her kid therapy. A mom who couldn't even speak without a stutter for ten months after the shooting. A mom who had to walk with a cane until last month. A mom who is still scared of her own shadow.

* * *

My mom's name is Naomi. I am her miracle baby. She wasn't supposed to be able to have kids. I was also a surprise. Mom named me after a Kenny Rogers song. She says she liked the way "Ruby" went with my last name, Gold. A precious name for her precious child. My dad left Mom before I was born. He wasn't ready for the responsibility of a kid. I feel weird even calling him my dad. He was never a dad. He was Daniel. That's it.

Mom calls me a blessing. At least she used to.

* * *

Doctor Sanderson says that my B word is powerful. She said when I say the word my face changes. Bullets. It's a hard word to say.

They are just so fast.

BALLOONS

NAOMI

"All the adversity I've had in my life, all my troubles and obstacles have strengthened me... You may not realize it when it happens, but a kick in the teeth may be the best thing in the world for you."

Walt Disney

I went to a conference yesterday. It was a work requirement. Nothing special. A typical conference with a presenter and lots of participants. What made this conference different from all other conferences I have attended (and, I have attended many a conference), was the balloons. There were balloons at this conference. I used to have no problem with balloons. I actually liked them. I still like *The Red Balloon*. I took Ruby to the play when she was little. I love the Mickey Mouse shaped balloons at Walt Disney World. But, balloons are different now.

The presenter started by asking all of the participants to blow up a balloon. There were 200 participants. That meant 200 balloons. Then she asked everyone to get with a partner and pass one balloon back and forth. So, we paired off and chose one balloon out of the two we had among us. The other balloon, we dropped on the floor. That meant 100 balloons were on the floor of a conference room filled with 200 participants. Next, she directed us to pass the balloon back and forth using our hands, then our elbows, then our knees, then our toes. It was a fun game. It was supposed to emphasize teamwork. And it would have been great, except that with so many people passing balloons back and forth and with so many body parts and so many balloons already on the ground, it was a recipe for a very loud activity. All of a sudden, POP! The pop was followed by screams of surprise. Then another POP! Followed by another scream.

POP
Scream
POP
Scream
POP POP
Scream
POP POP POP
Scream

I knew it was balloons popping. I knew the screams were playful. I knew there weren't any gunshots. I saw the balloons. I blew one of them up myself. I knew in my brain that I was safe. I was OK. Everyone was just having fun. It was just a game at a conference. Harmless.

The presenter then asked us all to drop the balloons and jog in a circle. Now there were 200 balloons on the floor (minus the ones that were already popped, so maybe 150). 200 people jogging on a floor covered with 150 balloons.

POP POP POP POP POP POP POP POP POP POP POP

My heart raced. My palms were sweaty. My vision blurred. My breathing increased until I could barely catch a breath. I had to leave.

So, I did. I ran out of the conference.

I cried. I shivered in my car.

And…I felt like a failure.

CAR ALARMS

RUBY

"And as the wind gusted against those windows, I saw how, in an instant, I lost my shelter. This truth had hardly escaped me until then, far from it, but the clarity of that moment was overwhelming.
And I am still shaking."

Sonali Deraniyagala, *Wave*

About a month after the shooting Grandma thought it would be a good idea to take me and Mom to the ocean. "Ruby, you and your mom need to get away from the city for a while. Smell the salt water. Eat fish. Feed the seagulls."

Grandma meant well. She paid for the rented condo, bought all the food and even drove through a freak hail storm. But apparently post-traumatic stress disorder has a wicked mind of its own. PTSD is the kind of disease soldiers have after being in battle. I don't know much about it, but I do know that mom blamed her PTSD every time she fell to the floor and started crying like a baby.

She usually turned into a crazy mess after grandma locked the doors to her Saturn. Unlike our no-frills Kia, Grandma's car had a wireless door lock. For most normal families this wouldn't pose a problem. For my family, however, this was a major disaster, especially since the condominium complex had a parking garage. Have you ever heard a car alarm in a parking garage? It sounds like aliens attacking. We would be halfway to the elevator, mom would be *almost* laughing about a joke I made, our hands would be full of groceries and rented DVD's and a second later Mom would be in the fetal position, groceries scattered everywhere. The moment Grandma pressed that dreaded button and the car alarm sounded Mom would hit the deck. Every time.

Mom's whole body shook. She cried and she panted like a dog. It was embarrassing. I kind of feel bad about being embarrassed. But my mom was surrounded by peaches and halibut wrapped in white paper. She was crouched on the floor of the parking garage. Grandma stood with her car keys in her right hand and an expression of surrender on her face. This same scene played out over and over for a week. The groceries changed, but the rest stayed the same.

I wondered what kind of a mom was terrified of a car alarm. I wondered what kind of a grandma kept forgetting her daughter was terrified of the car alarm. But the more I thought about it, the more I realized that Grandma wanted to rescue Mom from her pain and Mom wanted to be rescued. She really did. They were both making the effort. Grandma would wait until things seemed normal and then she'd push the button. Mom would desperately try to compose herself after panicking. They just wanted to be able to make it to the elevator without making a scene. It was Mom's new gut reaction to loud noises that made it impossible. It wasn't anyone's fault. They were doing what Jewish moms do. They were trying to spare their children from pain.

CORTISOL

NAOMI

"We made friends with the shark which followed us today. At dinner we fed it with scraps which we poured right down into its open jaws. It has the effect of a half fierce, half good-natured and friendly dog when it swims alongside us. It cannot be denied that sharks can seem quite pleasant so long as we do not get into their jaws ourselves."

Thor Heyerdahl, *Kon-Tiki*

Cortisol is yet another hormone released in response to stress. This article-reading is proving beneficial. I am learning a lot. When I was at the conference and the balloons started popping, my adrenal gland released adrenaline (also known as epinephrine) and cortisol into my bloodstream. Interesting.

Common side effects of cortisol include shakiness, anxiety and sweating. Yes! Exactly how I felt at the conference.

Apparently, cortisol can also make you fat. I am not sure how scientific that is, but I have read it, or heard it, or maybe I made it up. All I know is, I feel fat and I am blaming the cortisol.

Dr. Willer (Ruby calls him my worry doctor), told me to stop reading so much. It increases my worrying. But I love to read. I love gathering information. Information is power.

* * *

This alphabetical journal is difficult. I wonder if it is as hard for Ruby as it is for me. Ruby is coming with me to my next session with Dr. Willer. He wants to meet her. I'm nervous.

DECEMBER

RUBY

"It is obvious that the war which Hitler and his accomplices waged was a war not only against Jewish men, women, and children, but also against Jewish religion, Jewish culture, Jewish tradition, therefore Jewish memory."

Elie Wiesel, *Night*

It's not December, but Dr. Sanderson says I need to pick a word that resonates with me. It is supposed to have meaning and contain specific memories. She loved Car Alarms. I think she will like December too.

I let her read my journal. She is a doctor, after all. And, I want that gift card.

The December after the shooting was one to remember. A December to Remember. If that isn't the name of a book or movie, it should be. First of all, Mom was too scared to put a menorah in the window. She didn't want to advertise that we were Jewish. This was the same reason she gave for ending our Shabbat dinners on the wrap-around front porch. The view of the sunset was not worth the possibility of a passing anti-Semite noticing our Sabbath candles and covered challah. Mom was so happy when we moved to our house on the beach. She taped a picture of a setting sun on the TV with the caption, "Our TV Set has been replaced with Sunsets". Tacky.

Second, some rabbi decided to give the airport a hard time about Christmas trees in a public space. He said they should either take down the Christmas trees or put up a menorah too. The airport stood behind their decision to have Christmas trees, arguing that they were "holiday trees".

Seriously?

The media covered this December debacle 12 hours a day until the airport finally took down the trees. Then they covered it 24 hours a day because the pro-Christmas tree community went wild. Jewish organizations started receiving hate mail and hate phone calls.

Mom's office, still on high alert after the shooting just months earlier, went into September 12th 2001 mode. Even long-time employees were hand-wanded before entering the building. Bomb-sniffing dogs randomly visited the parking garage and all packages were x-rayed before opening.

Mom came home every day in a near panic. When I asked her if she could visit my school to talk about Chanukah like she does every year, she said that "it might not be a good year" for talking about Chanukah.

Eventually the airport put the trees back up. They even put a menorah in the food court. But, the damage had already been done. Our family menorah was still safely wrapped in a blanket of tissue paper, tucked in a cardboard box, hidden in the shed by the side of our house. I still got presents. We still lit candles. But we did it all with the blinds closed.

Sometimes I wonder if this is all new or if it's been going on forever and I just didn't notice. Has being Jewish always been so difficult? Have people always fought about Christmas trees and hid their menorahs? Have there always been anti-Semites sending hate mail to strangers just because they're Jewish? Have there always been gunman terrorizing Jewish organizations?

It feels like all of this started a little over a year ago, when the first shot was fired at my mom's work. It feels like that was the beginning, and everything was just fine before then. But that wasn't the beginning. There's always been hate and violence and terror. It's just that now I'm looking for it.

Sometimes I think that I don't want to be Jewish anymore. I don't want to be Jewish if it means my mom keeps her Star of David in a box on her shelf. I don't want to be Jewish if it means I will always be afraid. After the shooting Mom said something to a reporter that made the headlines. She said she felt hunted. I don't want to be hunted. Maybe being Jewish isn't worth being a target.

But, how do you stop being something you are?

* * *

I went to visit Mom's Worry Doctor. That's not his official title but I think it fits. He asked me a bunch of questions about my mom and our relationship; if we spend a lot of time together, if we fight, how we've changed. It was weird. When I'm talking to Dr. Sanderson I forget that Mom is talking to a doctor, too. Sometimes I get so overwhelmed by everything I forget that I'm not the only one who feels lost.

* * *

I was right, Dr. Sanderson loved talking with me about December. She said that the holidays are a tough time for a lot of people, especially people who have survived trauma. She nodded her head and wrote a lot of notes on her notepad when I told her sometimes I don't want to be Jewish. She asked me if I could tell my mom that. No way! Mom would freak. She may not be religious, but Judaism is such a big part of her. She cleans the whole house before Passover and makes sure there isn't any bread. She even cleans out the car in case there are crumbs in the seats. She doesn't think anything will happen to her if she doesn't clean; she just does it because her mom did it and her mom's mom did it. I don't really know if that is a good enough reason.

* * *

I forgot to mention that Hailey, Dr. Sanderson's kid, is in my English class. I recognized her name when the teacher called roll. I haven't said anything to her yet. It's kind of weird that I talk to her mom about my problems. I wonder if they talk about me. That's a creepy thought.

DREAM

NAOMI

"The bomb is primed to go off at one twenty.
A time-check: one sixteen."

Wisława Szymborska, *The One Twenty Pub*

I had a dream last night that Ruby and I died. We went on a camping trip. It was our last day and we were packing up the car. There is a science to packing – heavy items on the bottom, lighter items on the top. Ruby handed me the blue tarp we use in case of heavy rain. I shut the trunk. I could feel the weight of the trunk door. I heard the click. I could smell the pine trees, the wet earth, Ruby's shampoo.

The moment I shut the trunk, the car began to move forward. I screamed at Ruby get in the car! Step on the brake! She ran alongside the car trying to keep up, but the road was downhill and the car picked up speed. It went faster and faster. Ruby tried. She really did. But, she just couldn't reach it.

We stood together, Ruby and I, and watched the car race toward the end of the road. Ruby noticed the gas tank at the same time I did. It was huge, the size of a single-wide trailer. Ruby's eyes widened. Mine must have too, but only for a moment. The car sped toward the tank.

When it hit, it was soundless. I saw the explosion. But I didn't hear it. At first I thought how unlucky we were. All of our camping equipment, my purse, Ruby's new sunglasses, my cell phone, Ruby's baby blanket all gone. Our car, our only mode of transportation, was gone in an instant. At first that's what I thought.

The cloud formed the moment the car hit. It rose upward like a mushroom cloud. I imagine the beauty of it reflected in our eyes.

Then it turned outward and raced toward us at an alarming speed. Fire and earth and particles of car coming, coming. Faster. I didn't even have time to think of Ruby.

The cloud hit me. It must have been hot. But I didn't feel the heat. It must have knocked me down, but I don't remember falling. I only remember being on the ground, on the dirt road, in the woods, in the fetal position. I curled into myself. My eyes must have been shut, but I remember orange. Everything was orange.

It didn't hurt. It tingled. My skin, from the top of my head to my toes, tingled. I knew intellectually that my flesh was being burned from the bone. I could sense the fat bubbling in the extreme heat. I knew my eyes must be melting – everything that was once me was quickly being turned to ash. It registered. It all registered. But all I thought was, *This is it. This is the end. The real end. This isn't a dream. This isn't survivable.*

But, how could this be? We were packing up to leave. We were almost on the road. I was planning on stopping for ice cream on the way home. I was already thinking of how many loads of laundry I was going to have to do. Then it came, the orange cloud. It engulfed us. It turned us to bone. All I saw was orange. All I thought was, *This is it. I'm going to die. Right here. Right now.*

I forgot Ruby was even there.

24

When I woke up I was shaking.

I've been thinking about the dream all day.

EVERYTHING IS MESSED UP

RUBY

"He thrusts his fists against the posts
and still insists he sees the ghosts."

Stephen King, *It*

I feel like I'm not really getting anywhere with this therapy stuff. According to Dr. Sanderson, my feelings are perfectly normal even though sometimes I feel like I am spinning out of control. She tells me to "stick with it" and keep writing.

Sometimes I feel like my mom that night I found her alone in the parking garage of the beach condo Grandma rented to get us away from it all. Mom was standing barefoot in her pajamas and robe, her arm extended straight in front of her, Grandma's car keys dangling from her hand. She took a deep breath, mumbled something to herself and pressed the wireless door lock. The car beeped loudly, the sound echoed throughout the garage. Mom stiffened. Her legs visibly shook.

"Mom? Are you okay?"

She looked at me with haunted eyes. "Even though I prepare for it, it still gets me. My mind knows it's only a car alarm, but my body thinks it's a bullet. I can't control my damn body. What's wrong with me?"

Mom wasn't really asking me. She was asking the universe, or God or something. Not me. But, I still answered. "Nothing's wrong with you."

That's not true. There were a lot of things wrong with my mom. She had almost died and now she was scared of monsters. But mom's monsters weren't the make-believe kind. They were real and still are. Sometimes I feel like mom's monsters haunt me too. I was never as scared of just being me as I am now.

Dr. Sanderson tells me I'm allowed to be scared. But I also have to be brave.

* * *

I asked Dr. Sanderson if she talks to her daughter about her patients. She said that would be a breach of doctor-patient confidentiality. I guess that means no. I still haven't told anyone Hailey is in my English class.

EVIL

NAOMI

"The world is a dangerous place to live,
not because of the people who are evil,
but because of the people who don't do anything about it."

Albert Einstein

Philosophers talk a lot about evil. Evil is defined in philosophy in mostly two ways. 1) Profoundly immoral and malevolent. 2) Wickedness, and depravity, especially when regarded as a supernatural force.

So, there's the everyday human kind of evil like Hitler. And then there's the supernatural evil like Satan. I don't know much about the supernatural.

But, Hitler, I believe. I don't believe *in* Hitler. But I know he was a real person. Someone who committed atrocious acts. Someone who is the closest thing to Satan on this earth that I can imagine. I guess I would define Hitler as evil. But, if I define Hitler as evil, do I run the risk of making him "the other".

Hitler was human. Just like me. Hitler was a living, breathing person. By accepting that, I have to accept that all people are capable of evil. We are, in essence, all evil. Some of us more than others, I suppose. Evil may come in degrees. But, if we are all human, then aren't we all evil? Is there anyone evil-free? Even Mother Teresa believed that suffering – even when caused by poverty, medical problems, or starvation – was a gift from God. Isn't that evil? Either evil from God or evil from Mother Teresa.

By defining someone as "the other" it makes it seem as if they are something that we could never be. But that's not the case. We are all capable of things we never thought possible.

After the shooting – the day that I want to forget, wish I could forget, but that I just keep remembering – I wanted the gunman to die. I wanted to kill him myself. I didn't care that he was a murderer and that if I killed him I would be a murderer too. That didn't matter to me. If I had the chance, I may have killed him. Does that make me evil?

FINALITY

RUBY

"Life is for the living.
Death is for the dead.
Let life be like music.
And death a note unsaid."

Langston Hughes

I once read an author who said that it wasn't death that scared him, but rather how long he was going to be dead. I never thought about the length of death before. People always talk about the length of life, but rarely death. Death is forever, and forever is too long to think about.

I don't ever remember being scared to die. Mom told me last night that she was never afraid to die until the moment when she thought she was actually going to die. She says that it wasn't like in the movies or in books where a character's life passes before their eyes. It was exactly the opposite. Nothing happened. Nothing, except for the realization that she was going to die a bloody, horrible death. As the shots got closer to her office, Mom decided to jump out of the window. She was sure she would die either by bullets or by splatting in the alley below. Either way, she was dead.

I've been wondering why my mom decided to share this information with me. Isn't she supposed to protect me? Now she tells me that the only thing that went through her mind as she was about to be shot was nothing. NOTHING. Not even me.

It kind of makes me feel like…well, nothing.

FORGOTTEN

NAOMI

"Life goes on if you're one of the lucky ones.
But we're still part of a secret club,
One we'd never willingly join,
With members who have nothing in common
except a time and a place."

Judy Blume, *In the Unlikely Event*

Have you ever eaten at a fancy restaurant? It could be any restaurant, really. But, in my mind, it is a fancy restaurant. The server brings your food plated in an exquisite way. It's all about the presentation. That first glimpse of the dish brings to mind famous art pieces. It is beautiful – almost too beautiful to eat. But, you do eat it. And it tastes as good as it looks. The flavors dance on your tongue. This may be the most delicious thing you have ever placed in your mouth. In twenty minutes, the dish is gone. The tastes linger for a moment, but then they too fade. In twenty minutes the work of the executive chef, sous chef, line cook, server, menu crafter, restaurant owner, and who knows how many others, has disappeared.

The finished product disappears the work.

There is so much work to be done in the kitchen before the dish is presented. And, all of that work is not seen by the diner. That's like life…isn't it? Who I am today is a product of all of my experiences. The work that went into producing me at this moment is not seen by those around me. People only see the outside, but not the work that went into forming every scar, every wrinkle, every gray hair. The full stories are left untold.

What if all of our stories were worn on our outsides? What if when someone looked at me they saw everything I have been through? What if they saw all of my dreams, all of my fears, my past, my decisions – those I am proud of and those that I am not – my strengths, my weaknesses? What if I saw all of this in others? Would we understand each other better, or would we melt away the mystery?

I guess what I am getting at is, I don't want the process that went into forming me to be forgotten.

I've said a lot about what I don't want. What do I want?

I want people to look deeper into each other. I want everyone to realize that there is more to every human being than what is readily apparent on the outside. I want the work behind the scenes, in the kitchen, to be appreciated – even if the work is not always known.

GOD

RUBY

"God dwells within you, as you."

Elizabeth Gilbert, *Eat Pray Love*

Some people write the word God with a dash for the "o". G-d. At least, some Jewish people do. This is because if the name of God is written on paper and the paper is thrown away or recycled or used as kindling or whatever, the name of God would be desecrated. I have never really understood this practice. I mean, I guess I respect it. I just don't understand it. God isn't really anyone's name. It's more of a concept.

My mom always described God by using the three letters G, O and D. She pretty much discards the G and the D, but she says the O is like the O in Holy. She says that she imagines stuffing everything holy and good and wonderful into that O and it grows bigger and bigger. Mom imagines God as a giant O filled with everything good. At least, that's how she used to imagine God. Since the shooting, she won't let me mention God or god or GOD or even G-d.

The last time we went to synagogue was for a back to school barbeque.

It was held outside on a sunny August day. Mom still used a cane and she couldn't speak very well because of her PTSD stutter. We were standing in line waiting for burgers when the cantor came over and grabbed mom by the arm. She hugged her and, with tears in her eyes, told Mom how she had just come from the hospital where she had visited the shooting survivors who had not yet been released. Mom tried to balance on her cane, with a plate of potato salad in her left hand as the cantor continued to grab Mom's right arm, telling her all about how hard it was for her to see everyone in the hospital.

She never asked about Mom. How could she not notice? Mom just stood there and nodded. She was silent. Her eyes brimmed with tears. I don't know if she was sad or in pain. Or both. When the cantor left, we got our burgers and took them to the car. We drove away and never went back.

I don't want to talk about God anyway. I'm not sure how or what I feel. Before the shooting I thought that God looked out for good people. But, my mom is good and so were her coworkers. They worked for a Jewish charity. They fed the homeless and cleaned up beaches. But some of them were shot and died and some of them were shot and lived, and some, like my mom, weren't shot but they are forever injured for a million other reasons. I don't want to think of my mom hiding from a Jew-hater.

She peed her pants.

I'm not supposed to tell anyone that.

Where was God?

GOD

NAOMI

"Exalted and hallowed be God's great name
in the world which God created, according to plan."

Mourners Kaddish

The *Mourner's Kaddish*, the Jewish prayer for the dead, pleads for "God's majesty to be revealed in the days of our lifetime." That's interesting considering this prayer has been around since the year 900. Supposedly, the first time mourners said the *Kaddish* prayer – or, the first anyone mentions it – is in the 12th century.

The first year of the 12th century was 1101. If we assume that a lifetime equals 100 years (which we know is not true, especially in the 12th century, but I need to pick a number and 100 is an easy one), then 900 lifetimes passed before the first year of the 21st century. 900 lifetimes. If we assume a lifetime lasts only 50 years, that number doubles.

That means, approximately 1000 generations have prayed that God's majesty be revealed to them. I'm not a Torah scholar or a mathematician, but – according to my calculations – this prayer is not working. And, ironically, the prayer promises God's majesty both "speedily" and "imminently". Like I said – not working.

The *Mourner's Kaddish* in Aramaic is *Kaddish Yatom* or, *Holy Orphan*, "Holy" being the prayer and "Orphans" being the ones who say the prayer over the dead.

The Orphan's prayer.

It's haunting.

The prayer blesses God's name to eternity. Blessed, praised, honored, exalted, extolled, glorified, adored, lauded. It's like a prayer thesaurus.

While the dead lay lifeless, the grieving praise God and trust in His great plan.

HOWEVER

RUBY

"We delight in the beauty of the butterfly, but rarely admit the changes it
has gone through to achieve that beauty."

Maya Angelou

Dr. Sanderson says that whenever I am about to say 'but', I should
replace it with 'however'. It's supposed to expand my thinking. 'But' is a
stop sign. 'However' is a yield sign. I wonder if she knows I don't drive yet.

I thought of a lot of words I could write about that begin with 'H'. Hate.
Horrible. Horrendous. Horrid. Okay, I guess those last three are pretty
much the same.

Of course, there is Happiness. Hope.

Hell.

According to the Oxford English Dictionary, 'however" is defined as,
"used to introduce a statement that contrasts with or seems to contradict
something that has been said previously". 'But' is defined as, "used to

introduce something contrasting with what has already been mentioned".

What's the difference?

Is Dr. Sanderson really trying to expand my thinking or is she giving me busy work to occupy my mind? Is replacing 'but' with 'however' like rearranging deck chairs on the *Titanic*? Pointless?

So, 'however' fits because I have no idea why I'm doing this exercise. And, since so much of life seems pointless, I have given up hate, happiness, and Hell for however.

* * *

Sorry. I guess I'm just in a crappy mood. Some days I feel like things are getting better and then it all goes to Hell. Yesterday Mom laughed at a joke I told her. She laughed so hard she had tears in her eyes. I was laughing along with her. It felt good, until Mom's laugh-tears turned to real tears and she locked herself in her bedroom. Does she know I can hear her cry? Even when she turns on the shower and the TV and tries to hide it, I can hear her. It sounds the same every time. Dr. Sanderson says it's normal to take three steps forward and one step back. I feel like we're taking one step forward and three steps back. It's exhausting.

We laughed though. For a little while. It was almost like nothing had ever happened to take the laughter away.

HATE

NAOMI

"The opposite of love is not hate, it's indifference.
The opposite of art is not ugliness, it's indifference.
The opposite of faith is not heresy, it's indifference.
And the opposite of life is not death, it's indifference."

Elie Wiesel

Sometimes I hate him so much.

The gunman. That's what Ruby and I call him. Why give him a name? He lost his name the moment he picked up a gun.

I hate him because he's a murderer. I hate him because he's a life-destroyer. I hate him because he made me a different person.

I hate him for taking away my motherhood, my laughter, my innocence, my daughter's innocence, my trust, my understanding.

I go to work every day. And every day I see his face. In every doorway. In every corner. I don't know how long I can do it – return to work. I may need another job.

Sometimes I hate him so much.

* * *

I started wearing my Star of David necklace again. Sometimes I think I wear it just to spite him, and other times I am sure I wear it because I miss that part of myself.

ISRAEL

RUBY

"War is what happens when language fails."

Margaret Atwood

I know as a Jew I am supposed to support Israel, but – I mean, however, – I don't really know anything about Israel other than what's in the Torah and on CNN. The man who shot up the Jewish charity where Mom works was mad at Israel. That's what he yelled the whole time he was shooting. He said he wanted America to stop supporting Israel.

Back when I used to go to synagogue, we hosted an Israeli Café in Hebrew school. Parents, relatives, and friends were invited to attend. Students served falafel and Israeli salad and hummus and tahini. We ordered and served in Hebrew. The menus were in Hebrew. Morah Tamar played Israeli music. Israeli flags and posters of Haifa and Eilat and Tel Aviv adorned the walls. It was wonderful.

I know that some people hate Israel. I don't. I want to go someday. I want to go to the beach and the desert. I've heard Israel is beautiful. It is part of our earth – just another land with sand and trees and people. Why can't grown-ups get along? Why can't they stop shooting and start being nice? That's what they teach kids, right? Why don't they follow their own advice?

Did the gunman realize he wasn't in Israel? He was mad at Israel. But he didn't shoot Israel, he shot Jews in America. He shot people who weren't even Jewish. He shot mothers and sisters and best friends. He shot people who had never even been to Israel.

I

NAOMI

"It is a sin to write this. It is a sin to think words no others think and to put them down upon a paper no others are to see."

Ayn Rand, *Anthem*

I remember when I was in the hospital, after I had given birth to Ruby, I didn't want to leave. The nurse came to me one day with discharge papers and I argued with her.

I can't leave, I said. *I'm not ready.*

In the hospital when Ruby cried the nurses brought her to me. I fed her. They took her away and I slept. When I was hungry, they would feed me. When I was tired, I would sleep. When I needed extra fluids, they would hook me up to a machine and nourish me. I loved the hospital. They took care of me and they took care of Ruby. If I left the hospital I would have to take care of Ruby alone, and no one would take care of me. I didn't understand why the nurses and the doctors and hospital administrators didn't understand that I could not leave.

I left.

I think, the thing about hospitals is, you can't stay in them just because you want to. As Nurse J said to me, "This ain't a hotel, sweetie."

I am a mother. Being a mother has always been my favorite job. My most important job. I am a mother before all. But, lately, I feel like I need a mother. I have one, of course. She's a great mother. But, I can't ask her to move in with me and Ruby and take care of us. I mean, that's *my* job.

I want a fake mother. A rent-a-mother. Someone who will sweep in, make everything better and only leave when my entire world smells of lavender and eucalyptus and Ruby has graduated valedictorian and everything is as perfect as perfect can possibly be (given the imperfect circumstances of life).

If you ask a real mother for help, you feel guilty. A fake mother doesn't require guilt. A fake mother is perfect.

Given the imperfect circumstances of life.

JEWISH

RUBY

"You cannot do a kindness too soon, for you never know how soon it will
be too late."

Ralph Waldo Emerson

I am Jewish. That feels good to write. There may be horrible people out
there who will hate me because I'm a Jew but they would hate me if I were
a thousand other things, too. So, I am Jewish.

Mom is wearing her Star of David again. She keeps it on a long chain
and tucks it under the collar of her shirt. At least she's wearing it. It's not
the same one she used to wear. That one broke off when she jumped. The
police had to take it in for evidence. She has it back now but she keeps it in
a box on her shelf. The new Star of David she wears is from a stranger.

When the media found out that Mom's necklace broke off when she
jumped, they had a heyday. The media loves symbolism; a Jew who loses
her Star of David while fleeing from a murderer? That's pretty symbolic.
The story aired and a flood of messages, prayers, and Stars came pouring in.

Mom got packages, letters, envelopes and plenty of necklaces. Complete strangers sent her Stars to replace the one she lost and to show their support. Some were silver, others gold, my favorite was a round mosaic charm with the star etched in the center. Mom gave me one of the Star necklaces, a tiny silver one with a purple gem in the middle. I don't wear it; not because I'm afraid, because I want to keep it safe.

Chesed in Hebrew means acts of loving kindness. I don't know if it's thinking about these acts of loving kindness that help me feel less afraid of being Jewish or if it's my mom being proud and brave enough to wear her star again. All I know is that I'm starting to remember that people can be wonderful and kind and loving. It makes me feel good. I hope it lasts.

* * *

I told Dr. Sanderson that Hailey is in my English class. Now she wants to get us together. I don't think I have anything in common with this girl. For one, I don't have any close friends this year since my two best Middle School friends went to St. Margaret's Christian. Hailey is surrounded by friends. I eat lunch alone on a bench outside and read. Hailey eats lunch with about a hundred people at a table made for ten. I am getting an A in English and I am pretty sure Hailey is failing. Dr. Sanderson seems to think I could be a good "balance" for Hailey. Doesn't this breach some kind of doctor-patient thing?

* * *

Mom just got off the phone with Dr. Sanderson. It's done. We are meeting them for dinner on Christmas Eve. Ugh.

JEWEL

NAOMI

"It is not unlike me that in heading toward the west
I should travel east."

John Steinbeck, *Travels with Charley*

Ruby was going to be named Ruth. I called her Ruth all through my pregnancy. Ruth was my great aunt's name. I never knew my great aunt, but all my life I heard how wonderful she was. How altruistic and self-sacrificing. She was the epitome of generosity. She died years before I was born, but her name lived on at family dinners, in conversations late at night after the kids had been put to bed. Ruth. She was the one who gave up everything to raise her siblings after her parents had died. Ruth. She was the one who traveled across the ocean with the little ones in tow to a new world. Ruth. She was the one who never married, who never had children, who always put everyone else first.

It wasn't until I saw Ruby's face in the hospital that I realized I didn't want her to be Ruth. Ruby's shining screaming face, her strong lungs, her bright eyes. My child would never sacrifice everything for another.

The name Ruby didn't come to me right away. I was holding her, nursing her, listening to the radio when a song came on – Kenny Rogers. I didn't even like Kenny Rogers. But, I loved the name. Ruby. A shining, sparkling, bright jewel in my life. Ruby. It was perfect.

* * *

Dr. Sanderson's daughter, Hailey, is in one of Ruby's classes at school. How amazing is that? There is no better friend for Ruby than the daughter of a therapist. I think. They even invited us for Christmas Eve dinner. For the first time in a while, I feel excited.

KNOWLEDGE, *A POSTERIORI*

RUBY

"It was better to know the worst than to wonder."

Margaret Mitchell, *Gone with the Wind*

There are twenty definitions for knowledge in the *Dictionary of Philosophy*. My favorite is: knowledge, a posteriori – knowledge derived from sense experience.

Do you really know anything until you experience it for yourself? When my grandma came to pick me up at summer camp I knew something was wrong.

"I'm on the emergency pick-up list," she told the woman behind the front desk.

Emergency?

My mother picked me up from camp every day in the summer. The only reason my Grandma would leave work and drive two towns over to pick me up was if something was wrong with Mom.

Here it is. This is when it happens. The knowledge, a posteriori.

The paper on the art table shuffled. The water in the watercooler bubbled. The air outside was warm compared to the air conditioning inside, and I could smell the sea as the door closed behind my grandma. Her eyes were flat. The sun created a line across the floor, right in front of her shoes. Someone rushed in front of me – a kid on his or her way to snack. Grandma tried to smile. Her lips stopped short in a sort of pained look. I dropped my Junior Navigator's journal. Something was wrong.

My mother is the only person I know who reads books on the *Titanic* before going on a cruise. She says it's so she knows what she's getting herself into. Knowledge is power. However, knowledge isn't always in the right hands. The *Titanic* received six warnings about ice before she hit the iceberg that sunk her. Six warnings! If my mother had been warned six times of a shooting, she would have stayed home that day.

* * *

I don't know how I feel about Hailey. When we went for dinner on Christmas Eve I ordered the steak, she smiled at me with this half smile and then ordered a salad. Then she made a big deal about telling the waiter that she was a vegetarian and there could be no meat on her salad and nothing that touched meat could touch her salad or even be near her salad. Mom made the mistake of asking how long she had been a vegetarian. Hailey never really answered her, but she did tell us all about a video she saw with chickens in tiny cages and cows with their heads in boxes and slaughterhouses and lots of other disgusting stuff I didn't need to hear about before eating. I ate my steak like a hungry hyena though. Just to show her. I don't think she really cared. But I bet she'll get a laugh over it with her hundred friends at school while she drinks her organic, vegan smoothie from France.

Hailey gave me a necklace, even though I don't celebrate Christmas. Mom thought it was just the sweetest thing ever and kept saying how thoughtful Hailey was and how Dr. Sanderson raised such a delightful

daughter. I didn't get her anything. The necklace is a gold angel. I don't know what to do with it. Not only do I *not* celebrate Christmas and Chanukah was weeks ago, I also don't believe in angels.

Do you think she expects me to wear it to school?

KINGDOM

NAOMI

"After every war
Someone's got to tidy up.
Things won't pick
Themselves up, after all."

Wisława Szymborska

When I was in my twenties, I sort of fell into charitable work. Since then, I always thought I would be working for a charity for the rest of my life. I love helping people. I really do, I'm not one of those people who just says that.

At age 21, I applied for a job at a Jewish food pantry. The pantry wasn't just for Jewish people, it just happened to be run by a Jewish charitable organization and most of its donors were Jewish. I was hired not because I had any experience, but because I was Jewish.

Before being hired at the food pantry, I was working as a telemarketer convincing people in the Midwest that they had been selected to receive a Bahamas vacation. We couldn't say they won it, because they didn't. They were selected. Everyone who wrote their name on a piece of paper and stuck it in the box at the local drugstore or church or pub or old people's home was selected. All they had to do was fork over their credit card number.

I wish I could say I quit when I found out it was a scam, but I didn't. I owed too much in student loans.

Plus, I was pregnant.

I needed the money.

At seven months pregnant with a belly that looked like nine months I finally told my manager that I had had enough. No more scamming innocent people. No amount of prayer could wipe my conscience clean. So I took a job at the food pantry. I figured maybe doing some righteous work would help in the karma department. And, if there was a God, I certainly wanted a little light to shine my way. I was, after all, about to be a single mommy.

I barely made enough for prenatal vitamins, but it was worth it. I learned important things about myself. I love helping people. I have a great sense of humor. I'm resilient, and I can make countless dinners using expired matzah! I never thought that, years later, I would use that same food pantry to feed my own child.

Eventually, Ruby thought of the pantry as the grocery store. By the time she was old enough to really make the connection, I had a decent paying job at another Jewish charity and we no longer needed to eat other people's canned goods. This Jewish charity helped people in different ways, like funding desert irrigation and clean water initiatives. I loved that work. I mean, I love that work. It's what I still do.

Since the shooting, it's been harder. I still see the blood on the carpet and the walls. I still hear the screams and the cries.

Everything is cleaned up, of course. It looks like a brand new building. A designer decided that an open floor plan would be better so they tore down the offices and put up cubicles. A kingdom of cubicles. I really liked my office. My office window saved my life. Now, I am far from a window. I couldn't make it to one if someone started shooting. There is nowhere to hide either. Not in this open floor plan design.

It's pretty sad that I am concerned about hiding places at work, but it's my new reality.

LIFE

RUBY

"Even if a man lives many years, let him enjoy himself in all of them, remember how many the days of darkness are going to be. The only future is nothingness!"

Ecclesiastes, chapter 9, verses 7-10; chapter 11, verse 8

The Talmud says that God created humans on the sixth day so that we should be reminded that the gnats preceded us in the order of creation.

Is that supposed to humble me? Honestly, it makes me feel like dirt. Is that what I am? Dirt? Less than a gnat? I know that's not what the Talmud implies, but everything lately makes me feel like less than what I am.

Life is supposed to be fun. Life is supposed to be fulfilling. So, why are so many people unhappy? When I am an adult – an official adult, not the Bat Mitzvah kind – I am going to do what I love. Maybe I'll be a writer, or own an ice cream store. Or maybe I'll run an amusement park or invent a new flavor of popcorn. Whatever I do I will do something that makes me happy. I am not a complete idealist. I know that I need to make money if I want to have a house and eat and raise children. But, I don't see why I can't make money doing what I love. Or, at least, something that doesn't make me miserable.

I guess the thing that confuses me most about life is why people live it as if they are going to either live forever or get a do-over. It doesn't seem that most people really think this is it – this is their one chance to make it right. If they did, wouldn't everyone treat each other with kindness and respect? Wouldn't people smile more and not worry so much about fitting in, being cool or arguing about politics and religion.

Dr. Sanderson says I ask a lot of questions. I don't see anything wrong with asking questions. She says it's not bad to ask questions unless all I do is ask and never offer solutions. So, here is solution number one to the question, how can I make my life better: laugh more. I intend to laugh at least fifteen times a day. I found a joke website and I will read jokes and guffaw until my side hurts. I read that laughing triggers endorphins, the body's natural feel-good chemicals. I could use some feel-good chemicals right about now.

LYING

NAOMI

"Her counting ability came naturally from her mama. It was Mama who was always figuring up and weighing – bags of flour left; spoons of sugar; dozens of eggs needed; rows of stiches remaining; how many miles to the city; how many different trains to catch; how many days the nest egg would stretch; how much a pound, a yard, a piece, a week."

Breena Clarke, *River, Cross my Heart*

"What do you do?" I was asked that by a parent of one of Ruby's friends. I should know better than to volunteer at school events. I hate them. I am always on edge and I don't really like talking with people, but I can't just let Ruby's school years fly by. I mean, I need to be involved in some way. Right? So, I volunteered to serve pie on pi day. It's supposed to be a fun way to meld math with dessert. I was standing at the table serving pie alongside another parent when there was a lull in the pie line.

"I'm Grant," he said, "Dillon's father."

"Naomi. Ruby's mom."

"Oh yeah, sweet kid. So, what do you do?"

What do I do? Well, for the past year I have been waking up every morning, putting one foot in front of the other, somehow making it to work, and returning at night to have a fitful sleep until the next day.

I don't tell him that.

I raise that sweet kid of mine when, half the time, my mind is shattered.

I don't tell him that.

I do therapy. Is that what you mean? I talk to someone about my emotions and fears and why I hate doing stuff like serving pie and talking to people.

I don't tell him that either. What I do tell him is the truth.

"I work at a Jewish charity."

"Oh yeah, which one?"

And this is when I know exactly what is about to happen. Why didn't I say I was a stay-at-home mom or a grocery cashier? I could be a horse jockey or the person who paints the lines in the middle of the road. I mean, I'm pretty smart. I could come up with any profession. An astronaut? Sure. *When I return to earth, it takes a while to get my land legs back. Ha, ha, ha!* Or what about, *I'm sorry. I can't tell you what I do. That information is classified.* But, no. I chose none of those possibilities. I chose the truth. I told him which Jewish charity. And the rest is like a worn-out script.

"Wasn't that where…?"
"Yes."
"Oh my God. Were you there when…"
"Yes."
"Were you shot?"
"No."
"Did you know…"
"Yes."

Sometimes there are follow-up questions, "Did you see…?", "How did you get out?", "Were you scared?"

Or worse, "Did you fight?"

Then the platitudes:
"You survived for a reason."
"God has a plan for you."
"What doesn't kill you, makes you stronger."

Grant's was just as original. "Well, God never gives us more than we can handle."

Thanks, Grant. Now it all makes sense.

I never did ask Grant what he did. I found out later from Ruby. Turns out, Dillon's dad is a pastor.

Of a church.

Maybe I should ask Grant why God's plan for me included a shooting.

I really hate interacting with people. It always ends the same way. Next time, I'm lying. Next time, I'm an astronaut.

ME

RUBY

"There is nothing either good or bad, but thinking makes it so."

William Shakespeare, *Hamlet*

Rabbi Simeon ben Eleazer said that people should be as supple as the reed and not rigid as the cedar. When wind blows upon a reed, it bends. When the winds are still, it remains upright. The cedar, however, does not bend. As soon as the wind blows, it is uprooted and it collapses.

I want to be like the reed. I strive to be like the reed. I feel the wind blowing and I want to bend. I want to be flexible. But, I feel as rigid as the cedar.

* * *

January sucks. All the trees are dead. Mom says they aren't really dead, they are just hibernating or whatever. They sure look dead.

* * *

It's been one year and six months since the shooting. It's like I have a new calendar in my head. Everything falls into before the shooting and after the shooting. One year and six months ago I was still supple as the reed, able to be awed by the wind. It takes a lot to awe me now.

* * *

It's hard to laugh in January.

METAPHOR

NAOMI

"If a picture is worth a 1,000 words,
a metaphor is worth a 1,000 pictures!"

Thomas J Shuell

The essence of metaphor is understanding and experiencing one kind of thing in terms of another. I have found myself talking in metaphors lately. Today, Ruby asked me if I had a headache. I have been rubbing my temples all day. I do have a headache, but it wasn't enough to just say, "Yes, I have a headache." I felt the need to compare it to something in order for her to really understand the pain of the headache. So I said, "It's like the fluid in my brain has been replaced with gasoline and lit on fire." Ruby's response was to tell me to stop being so dramatic. Why the hell was I so dramatic? I could have just said yes and asked Ruby to get me some aspirin. But no. I had to compare my pain to a fiery inferno.

In a way I feel as though I have lost my ability to communicate in simple terms. It is suddenly very important to me that people understand what it is I am trying to say. I want people to get me. I feel the need to state and restate and clarify and speak metaphorically so that the world is sure to get how really, really painful this damn headache is.

Actually, that's not true. It's not the world that I want to understand me. It's Ruby.

I'm an awful mother. I need Ruby to understand *me*? I'm the mother! I should be trying to understand her. How does she feel? Why am I so self-involved? It's like I survived a lion attack and all I can think about is the lion and I'm ignoring my chicks in the nest.

What am I talking about? Am I a bird in this scenario? A bird attacked by a lion? Where is this even coming from? This is what my brain is doing to me right now. It's tricking me, confusing me. I don't trust my own brain!

Metaphors – something you use when you can't say what you're really thinking.

Because, what I'm really thinking is too scary to say.

NEW

RUBY

"The diameter of the bomb was thirty centimeters
and the diameter of its effective range about seven meters, with four dead
and eleven wounded."

Yehuda Amichai, *The Diameter of the Bomb*

I want to start something new.

On the one year anniversary of the shooting Mom and I attended a service. She was asked to read a poem by an Israeli poet, Yehuda Amichai. The poem was about a bomb. The bomb was small, but the devastation it wreaked was huge. It's like if you throw a stone into still water. The ripples move outward, affecting the water all around it, even the water that was not disturbed by the stone. That's what the poem was about. Instead of water, though, it was people who were affected.

Bullets have a ripple effect. They hit a place and they ripple. It doesn't even have to be you. They shatter lives and hope and innocence.

I can ripple. Dr. Sanderson says I can. The force that I put out there in the world can ripple out much farther than I can dream. I can choose to put forth a negative ripple, or a positive one. I talked to Mom about it. She says she wants to ripple too. So we are. We are choosing to send out positive waves into the universe. Mom says that we can create a new future for ourselves, a healthy future. When she says things like that, she smiles and almost looks like my mom before the shooting.

It feels good to think about doing something new – rippling. It's even fun to say!

Just to show what an amazing rippler I will be, I am going to invite Hailey to the mall to celebrate my birthday. I will be fifteen. A new year and a new me! Ripple, ripple, ripple.

NAMES

NAOMI

"To misname things is to add to the misery in the world."

Albert Camus

Sometimes I wonder if the way I see the world is the way the world really is. Everyone has a story and everyone's story informs the way they see the world. I get that. But sometimes I wonder if my story has affected my vision to a point of no return. Do you know what I mean by that? I am scared that maybe I will never see the world in the same way again. Will I always see everyday things as possible dangers?

Leo is a Holocaust survivor. He lost his wife and his daughters to the flames. When he was liberated, he emigrated to the United States of America, met a woman, married her and lost her to cancer three years later. Leo lives in an apartment alone. He rarely goes out. The agency I work for delivers holiday meals and, occasionally, soup and challah. Leo is scared to leave his apartment. He has lost not one but two wives to things he could not control, he could not fight. He lost his daughters to hatred. Leo tells the social workers that he has no desire to leave his apartment. He has everything he needs right where he is. They know better, but what are they going to do? Leo is old. He is set in his ways. They don't think he will

71

change. I think Leo is scared. Leo did not write his story; Leo's story has written him. At least, that is how he feels. I could be wrong. But, sometimes I see pieces of Leo in myself. That scares me.

I had a philosophy professor in college challenge the class to prove that the color blue was blue. When the class began to identify blue objects around the room he questioned, "But what if what you see as blue, I see as red? Is it still blue?" What if everything I see, someone else sees differently? What if my own reflection in the mirror is not what I present to the world? A student in that philosophy class eventually stated that the name of the color did not matter, however we saw it was the way we saw it. Period. But I think names do matter. The names we give to things hold weight. How we label something says as much about the labeled as it does about the labeler. So to misname something is akin to sentencing an innocent person. Names stick. Labels matter.

Gunman. Victim. Survivor. Shot. Injured. Dead.

Labels matter.

OMNISCIENCE

RUBY

"If you cannot even look at the sun, which is just one of God's attendants," said Rabbi Joshua, "how do you presume to be able to look at the divine presence?"

Babylonian Talmud

Rabbi Akiva said, "Everything is foreseen, yet freedom of choice is granted; in mercy is the world judged; and everything is according to the preponderance of good works." I'm not sure I understand Rabbi Akiva's words. If God plans everything out, then what does it matter how many good deeds someone does? I could do good deeds my whole life and then end up getting hit by a bus or shot at my desk.

Rabbi Joshua explains God as something we can never see clearly. Is this God? An invisible force that plays us like puppets? I learned all this stuff in Synagogue School. I can't believe it is still in my head.

Alfred Gwenne Vanderbilt survived the sinking of the *Titanic* only to perish on another sunken ship, the *Lusitania*, three years later. Did God really spare this man one watery grave in order to save him for another?

God doesn't make sense anymore. Before the shooting I thought that God was knowledgeable, powerful, and good. Now I don't know. Life seems too random, too disconnected, to be planned.

Last week I asked Mom if she still thinks of God as the O. Mom laughed.

"Do you think God is another letter?" I joked.

Mom actually seemed to think about it. "Maybe a question mark," she finally said.

Maybe God is a question mark.

* * *

Hailey can't go to the mall on my birthday. She will be with her dad that weekend. Oh well, maybe rippling that much was a reach anyhow. What would we have talked about?

OBSESSIVE

NAOMI

"Upon completing my journey, I realized that most of my fears were not
worth worrying about."

Stanley W. Beesley, *Vietnam: The Heartland Remembers*

Dr. Willer says I need to confront my fears. But first, I need to define
my fears.

Fear 1: People. You never know what people are going to do. People are
unpredictable. One minute he's a normal guy walking down the street and
the next he's shooting up an office building. One minute, they are just
passengers boarding an airplane and the next they are piloting it into an
office building. One minute, he's just a regular kid and the next he's a
murderer with a slew of little graves in his wake. These are people.

Fear 2: Ruby. I'm not scared of her. I'm scared of what I've done to
her.

Fear 3: Myself. I'm different. I know I am. Sometimes it feels as if my
brain has been swapped with someone else's. I don't even remember who I
was anymore. Who did I used to be? I think that woman is gone forever.

And, that scares me.

Fear 4: Being obsessive. I am fearful that I am obsessed with fear.

Fear 5: Everything. Breathing. Waking up in the morning. Life.

Everything. I am afraid of everything.

* * *

Dr. Willer says that I am not really afraid. There is a difference between fear and what I feel. You fear something that is actively happening. I felt fear during the shooting. Real, actual fear. What I feel now, he says, is worry. Worry is not fear. I am worried that I messed up my daughter. I am worried that I will never be the same woman I used to be. I am worried that this is all there is – for the rest of my life. And, if I "unpack" those worries (to use Dr. Willer's term), I find even deeper worries. I worry that I won't be able to survive this way. I worry that the world will just get darker and darker until it is only blackness. Have I reached a point of no return?

POSTAL, AS IN "GOING POSTAL"

RUBY

"Do not be afraid; our fate
Cannot be taken from us; it is a gift."

Dante Alighieri, *Inferno*

On August 20th 1986, Patrick Sherrill fired fifty shots at the Edmond, Oklahoma Post Office. He killed fifteen people. From that moment on the term "going postal" has been synonymous with "crazy". The really crazy thing is; Sherrill wasn't the first known person to shoot up a post office. He was the fifth.

Why did this type of crime make it to number five? If there is one thing I can do as a grown-up it will be to 'nip things in the bud'. That's what my grandpa used to say. It means to cut things off before they get too far. If I made all the rules, the United States Post Office would have learned to do psychological evaluations before hiring employees way before Patrick Sherrill got there. And, they would have an internal alarm system.

In school we do lock down drills. When the principal announces LOCK DOWN on the intercom, the teachers lock the doors, close the windows and blinds and we all huddle like scared mice against the wall or in corners or anywhere away from where bullets can fly in. Did they do drills at the Post Office? Probably not.

Since the shooting Mom always tells me to know my nearest exit. Sometimes she drills me. We'll be at the mall and she'll ask, "Where's the nearest exit?" At my school open house she was more interested in exit strategies than curriculum. "Don't forget, Ruby," she says, "your nearest exit may be a window."

I wonder when Mom will be able to enjoy a restaurant or a movie or anything without looking over her shoulder or scoping out emergency exits. She has always been the kind of person who counts the seats in front of her and behind her to the nearest exit on an airplane in case the plane fills with smoke and she has to navigate the aisle by touch. Now, she's even worse. She sits with her back to the wall, never to a door or window. She nearly hyperventilates in elevators. We have so many emergency supplies in our car, we could live in it for a month if there was an earthquake or some kind of National attack.

Dr. Sanderson says to give her time. She will get better.

Did the postal employees in Edmond, Oklahoma ever get better?

I heard people killed themselves after the Columbine school shooting. Why do people end their lives after surviving? Is it because they have seen the worst in people and can't get over it?

I know my mom is strong. She will be fine. So will I. Together, we will learn to see the good in people again. We will continue to go out to eat and to the theater and, one day, she won't be afraid. One day she will forget, even for a moment, about the shooting and she'll just be my mom again.

PTSD

NAOMI

"Sometimes I was seized by an inner fear
that was purely physical.
At such moments, I had nothing in common with my body."

Christine Arnothy, *I Am Fifteen – and I Don't Want to Die*

I am sitting in group therapy writing in my journal. I know I should be paying better attention but it's hard. This is a therapy group for people who have experienced trauma. Dr. Willer recommended it. This is my fifth group. Today, we are talking about PTSD. I feel like I have heard these people's stories over and over again. The one who was in a car accident. The one whose husband died while snow skiing. The one whose house burned to the ground after she fell asleep with a cigarette in her hand. The fire killed her cat. And then there's me, the one who survived a shooting.

PTSD. Post-Traumatic Stress Disorder. Here we all are sitting around a group of rectangle tables reading about PTSD. Another fun Wednesday night.

Diagnosis of PTSD involves four major criteria:

1. Re-experiencing – A brain with PTSD keeps returning to the trauma.

Check. The shooting plays over and over. Every day multiple times a day. Nightmares. Flashbacks. Memories.

2. Avoidance – Individuals with PTSD stay "numb" and are unable to get the same excitement when thinking about the future. These individuals also avoid any thoughts and cues that might trigger distress.

Check. It's hard to go back to work every day. I shake and feel nauseated just driving there. And, the future. What future?

3. Negative thoughts – If the trauma is remembered there may be distorted cognitions associated with the memory. Self-blame. Guilt.

If the trauma is remembered? Are they serious? How do I *not* remember the trauma? I survived. Why? Why didn't I do something to help my colleagues? Why didn't I fight? Why didn't I even think to call 911?

Check.

4. Increased arousal – Individuals with PTSD appear on edge.

On edge? Really?

Check!

I want to go home.

QUIXOTE

RUBY

"They must take me for a fool, or even worse, a lunatic. And no wonder, for I am so intensely conscious of my misfortune and my misery is so overwhelming that I am powerless to resist it and am being turned into stone, devoid of all knowledge or feeling."

Miguel de Cervantes Saavedra, *Don Quixote*

I read a book in school about a man who thought he was fighting giants, but he was really fighting windmills. Don Quixote was a fifty-year-old man who lived in a place called La Mancha. He read books about romance and chivalry which kind of made him crazy because he built this world in his mind where things weren't what they seemed.

One day, he decided to dress up in an old suit of armor and act like a knight in search of adventure. He renamed himself "Don Quixote de la Mancha," and named his skinny horse "Rocinante". He asked his neighbor, Sancho, to be his squire – kind of like a sidekick. He even promised Sancho his own island if he accompanied him on his adventures. Sancho agreed, and they snuck out of town early in the morning.

Eventually, the pretend knight and squire saw windmills in the distance.

Don Quixote was so determined to have his adventure that he immediately imagined the windmills to be ferocious giants that he and his trusty squire had to fight. He told Sancho, "Do you see over yonder, friend Sancho, thirty or forty hulking giants? I intend to do battle with them and slay them."

Sancho didn't see the giants – only windmills. But, Don Quixote couldn't be convinced and he charged towards a windmill at full speed. His lance got caught in the windmill's sail and broke. Later, Quixote replaced it with a tree branch.

Dr. Sanderson taped a copy of the page about windmills to my journal under "Q". She said I should consider how the story relates to me.

At first I didn't like the idea of Dr. Sanderson telling me what to write about. This is *my* journal. She told me I could still write whatever I want. She just wanted to "spark my creativity." Plus, I did tell her I was having trouble finding a Q word. And, she knows I love this story. Hailey and I were assigned the same book.

I get it. How Dr. Sanderson thought the story of Don Quixote might relate to me. It does. Quixote saw giants when there were only windmills. Sometimes we believe something is real, so we make it real, even if it's not. Sometimes we make things bigger than they are. Sometimes our monsters don't actually exist.

But what happens when they do exist? What happens if we really do see giants and everyone else just thinks they are windmills?

If Don Quixote trusted Sancho enough to bring him along, then why didn't he believe Sancho when he said there weren't any giants? And why did Sancho just go along with everything, pretending right along with Quixote that his imaginings were real?

Is that what the friends of the gunman did? Did they pretend that Jews were bad and that guns were good and that he should kill people and ruin people's lives just because they were too scared to stand up and say, "Hey, you're nuts!"

The newspapers said he had friends. His friends talked about the gunman to the papers after the shooting. They said he was "distant and remote", "discontent with society". They said they always knew something was different about him. Something was off. But they never said anything before the shooting. They never did anything. It was all in the aftermath.

* * *

Last summer Mom and I took a trip to the John Steinbeck museum. John Steinbeck is the author of one of her favorite books, *Travels with Charley*. She has two copies. One her dad (my grandpa) gave her before he died. The other copy has, "Not Dad's" written in Mom's handwriting in the upper left corner of the inside cover. It's like one is more important than the other and she has to separate the two somehow.

I don't know why she needs two copies. They look exactly the same.

We drove all the way to the museum and got there five minutes after it had closed. Mom left me in the car and walked up to the darkened windows. She stood with her face pressed to the glass, hands cupped around her eyes for about ten minutes until a security guard opened the door. I don't know what she said to the guard, but all of a sudden she clapped her hands, turned and waved to me and disappeared inside the museum. She was only gone a few minutes before she came out and ran to the car. When she got in it was like she had won the lottery or something.

"He let me see Rocinante! I even took a picture, see?" Rocinante was the name of the travel trailer John Steinbeck took across America with his dog, Charley. He named it after Don Quixote's skinny horse. The skinny horse that didn't hesitate when charging at a windmill. I think Mom loved that darn trailer so much because she imagined that one day she would pack up in a travel trailer just like that and leave everything behind. She wouldn't bring a dog though. She's allergic. I wonder if she would have brought me. I don't think she wants to do that anymore. The day mom saw Rocinante was one month before the shooting. I haven't seen her that happy since. I wonder if that security guard still works at the museum. I wonder if he thought Mom was nuts.

QUIET

NAOMI

"Thou shalt lie down
With patriarchs of the infant world—with kings,
The powerful of the earth—the wise, the good,
Fair forms, and hoary seers of ages past,
All in one mighty sepulcher."

William Cullen Bryant, *Thanatopsis*

When Ruby was little, I would put her in her crib and let her cry herself to sleep. It was so pitiful, so sad. She would inhale deeply. Then silence for what always seemed like too many seconds. Then a burst of a wail. If I didn't drown out her cries somehow, I would run in and rescue her from the torture. So, I used to go into the bathroom and start the shower. I would set a timer – one of the old-fashioned kitchen timers – to fifteen minutes. When the timer went off, I shut off the shower and checked on Ruby. By then, she was always fast asleep, her thumb in her mouth, tears already dried on her cheeks.

I never actually got in the shower. I just couldn't bear to hear her cry.

Now, when she's not home, it's too quiet. I don't like the quiet as much as I used to. I like to hear her. Her breathing. Her laughter. Her footsteps. Even the sound of the TV on in another room, knowing she is watching a show, settles my mind.

I need to hear her – to hear her living. It is a reminder that she is here with me. We are still together.

REVENGE

RUBY

"In spite of everything I still believe that people are really good at heart. I simply can't build up my hopes on a foundation consisting of confusion, misery, and death...
I must uphold my ideals, for perhaps the time will come when I shall be able to carry them out."

Anne Frank, *The Diary of a Young Girl*

I know that Anne Frank didn't live to carry out her ideals. She died – was murdered – at the hands of Jew-haters.

Sometimes when the world seems too overwhelming; when the buildings and the cars and the people are suffocating me, I look up. The sky is everywhere. It always was and maybe always will be. The sky sheltered Anne and it shelters me. Some shelters last longer than others.

I wonder if Anne ever looked up at the sky and thought of all the others that would come after her. It's strange to think that, after everything you've gone through, there will still be more to come.

* * *

The gunman is in prison. They found and arrested him after the shooting. We had to wait a long time before the court decided what to do with him. Mom told me today that he will spend his life in prison. I couldn't tell if she was glad or disappointed. Maybe she thought he deserved the death penalty. Maybe rotting in prison is worse.

I don't know what I want the gunman to do. I think my family and all the other families he broke deserve revenge. I just don't know what type of revenge.

We deserve to know that he'll be punished for what he did. Is that revenge?

Anne knew that she couldn't abandon her morals even though her world was in shambles. She had to continue to uphold her ideals in case she would ever get the chance to carry them out. I never wanted bad things to happen to people until someone made bad things happen to me. I don't think revenge is an ideal of mine. So maybe I don't want revenge. I just want this all to be over.

Mom says the best revenge is waking up every day and living. I think she believes that, because every morning when she wakes up now, she smiles. This is a new thing. She says it's to "trick" her brain to release the happy chemicals. I could tell her I know all about endorphins, but what's the point? Sometimes I think she likes to pretend I am still 12 years old. I will let her.

Mom smiles a lot more lately.

I think some of them are even real.

RAFT

NAOMI

"…whenever I saw the hunters with their long spears skimming over the water, I was angry, for these animals were my friends. It was fun to see them playing or sunning themselves among the kelp. It was more fun than the thought of beads to wear around my neck."

Scott O'Dell, *Island of the Blue Dolphins*

When I was a little kid, maybe nine or ten, I discovered a raft that had washed up on the beach. The small beach was on the shore of a lagoon near my house growing up. The beach was studded with mangroves and oyster shells. The raft was the perfect size for me. I could sit on it crisscross and use my hands to paddle around. I named the raft Suzie-John. I don't remember why I chose that name. Now, it seems like an odd name for a raft, but at the time I am sure it made perfect sense.

That raft took me so many places, even though it never left the 20 foot beach and never traveled more than five feet out to sea. But to me, Suzie-John took me to the Bahamas and Jamaica. We sailed to the Galapagos and might have even took a voyage through the Panama Canal. I don't remember if I knew about the Panama Canal back then. But, if I did, I guarantee I sailed through it on that raft

I imagined I was Karana from *Island of the Blue Dolphins*. I would lay strips of seaweed on the mangroves and pretend that I was drying abalone. I would peer out into the Intracoastal Waterway and imagine that the Sunday boaters going by were the Aleuts.

Those images are still so vivid in my memory. That raft was the world to me for months, until one day when I visited the lagoon and Suzie-John was gone. Probably washed back out to sea.

The funny thing is, Suzie-John was just a wooden pallet – the kind used on a forklift to support stuff. I made that ordinary pallet into something extraordinary.

It wasn't until I was an adult that I learned that the book, *The Island of the Blue Dolphins*, was inspired by a true story. Juana Maria was a Native-American woman who was left alone on San Nicholas Island off the coast of California from 1835 until her discovery in 1853. She is thought to have lived in a cave.

All those days that I pretended I was Karana – there was a real Juana Maria. Life is fascinating.

Life is precious.

SORRY

RUBY

"You're going to have things to repent, boy, Mr. John had told Nick. That's one of the best things there is. You can always decide whether to repent them or not. But the thing is to have them."

Ernest Hemingway, *The Nick Adams Stories*

After the shooting everyone was always sorry. Mom was sorry because she needed help. I was sorry because I couldn't help her. Grandma was sorry because she didn't know what else to do. Friends were sorry because they pitied us. The gunman's parents were sorry because their son shot people. Even strangers were sorry. I wonder if the gunman was ever sorry.

Mom would apologize a lot. Even when she hadn't done anything wrong. We would be standing in the kitchen, she would have her robe on and a cup of coffee and I would be eating a bowl of cereal and out of nowhere she'd stare at me, get all watery eyed, and say she was sorry.

I apologized a lot, too. The funny thing is that I don't think either of us ever expected an apology. We hadn't done anything wrong. We were just trying to heal. Maybe saying sorry helps you heal.

STETHOSCOPE

NAOMI

"Live in the sunshine, swim the sea, drink the wild air."

Ralph Waldo Emerson

You never know when a piece of knowledge will come in handy. For example…this is good… in 1816 Dr. Rene Theophile Hyacinthe Laënnec was 35 years old when he was walking in the courtyard of Le Louvre Palace in Paris. I imagine it to be morning. Cool. Beautiful. According to history, it was September. As he walked, he saw two children playing with a long piece of solid wood and a pin. One child placed an ear on one end of the piece of wood while the other scratched a pin on the opposite end. The scratch at one end was amplified at the other end. I imagine the children laughing. Laughing at their genius, and at the playfulness of the wood.

Later that year, Dr. Laënnec was called to treat a woman who was showing symptoms of a diseased heart. He knew he needed to listen to her heart, but placing his ear against her chest was going to be difficult for a variety of reasons. For one, she was a woman and placing his head on her breast was not something the doctor – in 1816 – thought appropriate. For another, she was obese. The rolls of flesh prevented him from being able to accurately get a pulse. It was at this time that he remembered those children in the courtyard. So, he created a crude horn and placed the trumpeted end against the woman's chest. *Voila*, the stethoscope.

Why is this moment important? Because you never know when something that may have seemed innocent at one time will become life-saving in another. I imagine the builders of the desk under which I hid during the shooting never thought that their creation would house a terrified woman. I imagine the architects who designed the building and who chose to place a window on the west side of an office overlooking a brick-lined alleyway never thought that their window would be an egress of freedom.

Perhaps someday, I will be able to share my story. The little things that maybe didn't matter at the time, but ended up having great importance. Maybe my story will help someone else. Maybe something I learned, something I went through, will aid someone else – help them along their journey. Wouldn't that be amazing?

TRUTH AND TITANIC

RUBY

"To thine own self be true."

William Shakespeare, *Hamlet*

In school today my English teacher said that William Shakespeare used words as ammunition. That word makes me cringe. Ammunition.

How many phrases are gun related?

Give it your best shot.
Shoot me an email.
In the line of fire.
I dodged a bullet.
That word is loaded.
That's a trigger.
Staring down the barrel.

Does anyone else notice this?

* * *

I am reading one of my mom's books about the Titanic if you haven't guessed. Why does she have so many books on the Titanic? Weird. Anyway, the book depresses me and uplifts me at the same time. During such despair there were still rays of hope, people who gave their lives for others.

Anne Frank saw that. She saw good from the depths of hopelessness.

When the Titanic was sinking, there were those who gave their lifebelts to others. The orchestra played until the deck was so slanted, they had to stop or they would slide into the frigid North Atlantic. They all did anyway. The wireless operator sent an emergency message even after he knew he was going to die. There were those who thought of others first. They tried to save as many lives as possible. They loaded lifeboats, shot off flares, led passengers through mazes of tunnels and stairwells.

If I am ever faced with the moment when I must be true to myself, I hope I am true to others. I hope that I will be able to serve humanity.

TODAY AND TOMORROW

NAOMI

"And if dead people aged, wouldn't it be a comfort?
Oh, it was their immunity to time that made the dead so heartbreaking."

Anne Tyler, *The Accidental Tourist*

Yesterday Dr. Willer asked if I have given any thought to what I want for my future. I haven't really thought about it. Ever since the shooting it feels like my whole world is confined to today. When I wake up in the morning I tell myself "just make it through today." Dr. Willer tells me to take things "one day at a time". I've been so focused on the present; there's been no room to think about the future.

Maybe I just don't want to think about the future. The future scares me. It shouldn't. I should be happy that I even have a future to worry about – and I am – but thinking about it is so overwhelming. How can I think about tomorrow when I can barely make it through today?

I know I need to plan. I need to think about Ruby's future too. She still has college ahead. Life goes on. Even when it feels like your world has come to a grinding halt, life still goes on. There are still bills to pay, groceries to buy, errands to run. Eventually, you have to prepare for tomorrow.

I used to be excited for tomorrow. There was so much I wanted to do. I suppose I can still do those things. I just need to find the motivation. I need to feel like there *will* be a tomorrow. One of my challenges is living with the knowledge that tomorrow is not guaranteed. I know that intimately. But, if I live like there might not be a tomorrow, I never look forward.

I must look forward.

USHPIZIN

RUBY

"The fear of death follows from the fear of life. A man who lives fully is prepared to die at any time."

Mark Twain

Hailey died. I thought about how to phrase that for a long time, but when it came down to actually writing it, that was all I could do. That's the truth. She died.

After the shooting when people spoke with my mother they would often offer their condolences. "We are so sorry for your loss", "They're in a better place", "I can't believe they passed".

It's all bull. People died. They didn't pass, or get lost, or fly off to some better world. They died. I'm sick of people sugar-coating tragedy.

I found out about Hailey in English. She was in a car accident with three other people. She's the only one that was killed. Kids at school are saying there was alcohol involved. Hailey wasn't driving. She was in the back seat.

When I told mom she screamed and called Dr. Sanderson. She got a voice mail and left a crazy message about how she's here for her and if there is anything we can do…blah, blah.

What can we do?

We didn't really even know her.

* * *

Dr. Sanderson's receptionist called Mom back. Dr. Sanderson is taking some time off. She offered to find us another doctor. I guess I don't have to write this journal anymore.

* * *

We had a memorial service at school. One of the other kids in the car died at the hospital. Dr. Sanderson was there. She didn't look at me.

I'm still going to write in this journal. Why not? It's not like I'm dead.

* * *

Ushpizin is Aramaic for guests. There's a story in the Torah where Abraham, Isaac, Jacob, Joseph, Moses, Aaron, and David come as guests to the sukkah on the festival of Sukkot. Each evening one of them is the main guest, invited into the sukkah and asked to bring the other ushpizin with him. It is also recommended that a poor person be invited each evening; otherwise the holy guests from the spiritual world will not stay since the poor person is meant to eat their portion.

It kind of sounds silly. And beautiful. Inviting friends and strangers, holy guests and poor people, into your space is beautiful in a way.

Ushpizin. It's a lovely word.

I wish I had invited Hailey into my space. She was a stranger and I never really gave her the chance to be a guest. Maybe I should have invited her to the mall on a day she wasn't with her dad. Maybe I should have sat at her table at lunch or invited her to my bench outside. Every once in a while.

I wonder if we could have been real friends. I wonder if that would have changed anything. Maybe Hailey did need balance like Dr. Sanderson said. I could have been that. I could have rippled more. My ripples didn't even reach Hailey.

UNCERTAINTY

NAOMI

"The Ojibway had never gone for headdresses and the totem poles
belonged three thousand miles away on the west coast of Canada,
but the tourists liked them so the band went along with it."

Mary Lawson, *The Other Side of the Bridge*

I should be used to someone being here one day and gone the next. I
have seen enough people die in my life to know that it can happen in a
moment.

You inhale, and you may never again exhale. At least, not consciously.

I was really upset when I heard that Hailey died. If upset is even the
right word. I feel that there should be a better way to describe how I felt
when Ruby told me. I screamed. I remember doing that. I called Dr.
Sanderson. Silly, I know. Like she would answer a phone call from someone
she barely knows after her kid just died. I guess I wanted to do something,
take some sort of action. Ruby went up to her room. She didn't seem as
shaken as I was.

* * *

I'm worried about Ruby. I think that is why I have calmed down a bit. I need to think of Ruby now. Hailey was in her class. They were beginning to become friends…maybe. I don't really know. I need to be more in touch with my daughter. I need to ask her more questions. I need to be more involved in her life. But, not overbearing. I don't want to push her away.

I can't lose Ruby.

She is my everything.

VAMPIRES

RUBY

"Death ends a life, not a relationship."

Mitch Albom, *Tuesdays with Morrie*

Why are vampires so popular all of a sudden? I don't remember people being so enamored with vampires until recently. Vampires seem to be everywhere. Books, movies, cartoons, TV shows…they are everywhere. Even clothing lines have gone "vamp". What is it about vampires that intrigues people so much?

I think it is the fact that they are supposed to be dead, yet they never really die. They walk around the earth in an almost-dead-but-not-quite-dead state. Vampires are cooler than zombies because vampires can still fall in love and get the girl or the guy and go to prom. Zombies are just disgusting, and eat people.

Real people are afraid to die and vampires allow them to think that maybe, in their fantasy world, there is an alternative. I don't know what I would do if a vampire gave me a choice to become immortal – to live forever – but only at night and only if I drink blood, or die like everyone else and face whatever unknown comes next.

Why did vampires take over our books, movies and malls? Because they are what we all want: to live forever. Well, most of us anyway. To never be faced with our own mortality. Death is scary. I know there are those people who say they aren't afraid to die because they know they are going to heaven or they'll be reunited with their loved ones or bask in the glory of God or whatever. But, do any of us really know? If the first day of school is scary because I've never met the teacher, then how can death not be scary? I've never met God. I've never been dead.

I guess Hailey knows.

If dead people can know things.

VIOLENCE

NAOMI

"About ten days or so
After we saw you dead
You came back in a dream.
I'm all right now, you said."

Thom Gunn

A man-made disaster sounds too homey to me. Like a homemade cake or a house made sauce. A man-made disaster like climate change or terrorism needs a better description. Don't you think? I recently learned of the term human-instigated. But I don't like that either. It sounds like people started it and then stepped away and let the disaster continue unencumbered by human interference.

I prefer the term human-created. It encompasses all people – women, men, children. Regardless of race, ethnicity, nationality, age, physicality. All humans. Creation is often attributed to God. Creation – a thing that only a god can do. God also does destruction. Insurance companies like to assign natural occurrences like a tree branch falling on a car, or a hail storm destroying someone's gazebo as an "act of God". As if God thought one day, "I don't like that gazebo. Or that Hyundai. I shall destroy both through an act of my creation."

Silly.

Human-created not only starts with the word human. It ends with the word created. We not only started it, we created it. We built it. Over time. In some cases, a lot of time. Creation often takes time. A lot of time. And, in that time we create more and more disasters. We build upon foundational disasters and create others on top of them. We build our houses along fault lines, resorts on beaches ravaged by tsunamis, ski lifts in avalanche zones. We see a disaster and create another. And another. And another.

Humans are unique in the fact that we can build great flying machines to sail along the winds and fly them into buildings inhabited by other humans. All creating.

We take the unintended violence and fill it with intent. Humans don't just make it, like a cake in the oven. We create it. We take something that is the building block of all matter – the basic make-up of our own selves – and we destroy entire cities. We decimate generations.

Humans have so much power.

I am human.

WORK

RUBY

"Never despair. But if you do, work on in despair."

Edmund Burke

After the shooting, those who weren't shot were asked to go back to work. Well, I'm not sure if they were actually asked or told. I mean, my mom went back to work even though she had to sit on an inflatable donut and she didn't sleep more than half an hour each night. But she said that work gave her a purpose. Odd. The same place she almost died now gave her life meaning?

The Chanukah after the shooting my school ran a fundraiser to adopt a family for the holidays. I remember seeing mom hoisting a large garbage bag out of the trunk of our car and dragging it into the house. Through the thin plastic I could see packages in Christmas wrapping. At the time I thought we had adopted a family. Later, I learned that she had unwrapped all the gifts and rewrapped them in Chanukah paper. We were the adopted family. Mom didn't go back to work because she wanted to. She did it because she needed to. Mom had to raise a daughter and she chose to return to the scene of a brutal murder day after day in order to care for me.

Dr. Sanderson has gone back to work, too. Today, we had our first session since Hailey died. She smiled a lot. It was weird.

She never mentioned Hailey. Not once.

Maybe Mom and I aren't so damaged after all. My mom is hardly a therapist and yet we've managed to make it through the worst times in our lives. Dr. Sanderson will make it through, too, but her daughter didn't. And now she's broken, just like me. Just like us.

Before the shooting, my mom ran marathons. She used to tell me stories of how she would get advice from other runners. "Run through the pain," they would say. Mom never listened. She said the real secret was to run *with* the pain. The pain doesn't go away; you just learn how to incorporate it into your stride.

I like that. The idea that dealing with pain isn't always waiting for it to go away, but sometimes making it a part of your life. Work with it.

Hailey ran marathons, too.

I can't tell if Dr. Sanderson is really as fine as she seems or if she's mending her broken lance with a tree branch. Is she going to break down one of these days? I wonder if she is seeing a therapist.

Hailey's picture is still on her desk. In it she's wearing her track uniform.

Smiling.

WORTH

NAOMI

"If a hiker gets lost in the mountains, people will coordinate a search. If a train crashes, people will line up to give blood. If an earthquake levels a city, people all over the world will send emergency supplies. This is so fundamentally human that it's found in every culture without exception."

Andy Weir, The *Martain*

It happens often. The word *only* makes my skin crawl. Not when someone is referring to a one-day-only sale or something like that. It bothers me when people use it to refer to human casualty. It's the opposite of what the local news channel does during a slow news day. The news team makes everything worse than it is. "A tree fell on First and Main. No injuries are currently reported, but who knows what could happen before the Tree Rescue Team arrives. We will keep you updated!" "Update! Tree Rescue Team in route to felled oak. Bystanders report a child on the sidewalk is flummoxed by the tree blocking her way home. Although we have reports of zero injuries currently, stay tuned for possible injuries and death which may or may not occur!"

This is the opposite. This is a different kind of spin. "*Only* three people died?" Someone actually asked me that today. Referring to the shooting, of course. *Only* three. I couldn't help myself. I felt myself cock my head, furrow my brow and say, "Only?"

"Oh, well, I didn't mean it like that."

"Then how did you mean it?"

"Well, I mean, it could have been worse."

"For who?"

"I don't know..."

"Because I am pretty sure the families of my colleagues who were murdered feel that it went pretty bad. I bet the word *only* doesn't mean the same thing to them as it does to you. Would it have been better if more people had been murdered? Would that make the crime more intense, more real, more relatable? Is this shooting not worth as much as others because *only* three people died? Is that how we rate shootings now?"

I know...I was a bit cruel. But, like I said, that word really makes my skin crawl. And the woman that used this word on me is a friend. She knows me. At least I thought she did.

And, I know people say stupid things. I know I need to forgive people. They just don't know what to say or how to react. I get it. But, *only*? Really?

Only six million Jews were murdered in the Holocaust? Oh, well that's better than seven million, right? *Only* 3,000 people were killed on 9/11? Whew! Way better than 4,000 or 3,050 for that matter. She was *only* raped? Not murdered? Well, lucky her!

When did we, as a society, become so jaded? When is any number of murders at the hand of a man who wanted to kill Jews not something to be disgusted by? The Talmud says, "Whoever destroys a soul, it is considered as if he destroyed an entire world."

I can promise you the gunman destroyed a world.

* * *

When the news came out about the accident, people used the word *only*. *Only* one teen died. *Only* Hailey. Then another teen died at the hospital and the word *only* stopped being used. Maybe two out of three teens dying tips the scale. Maybe that is it – it's not the number of deaths. It's the percentage.

XENOPHOBIA

RUBY

"Collective fear stimulates herd instinct, and tends to produce ferocity toward those who are not regarded as members of the herd."

Bertrand Russell, *Unpopular Essays*

Xenophobia is the irrational or unreasoned fear of that which is perceived to be foreign or strange. I had never heard of xenophobia until I asked Mom for help finding an 'X' word. All I could think of was X-ray and there really isn't anything deep I could write about that. Xenophobia is what breeds things like anti-Semitism and genocide. And it's not just directed at Jews. People die because of who they are every day.

In 1957 more than 1,000 paratroopers from the 101st Airborne Division and a federalized Arkansas National Guard protected nine black students integrating Central High School in Little Rock, Arkansas. Over a thousand people had to protect nine high school students just because of the color of their skin. People screamed at them, spit at them and told them to go back to Africa where they belonged. They called them horrible names. How could people be so cruel?

I see on the news other countries where there are civil wars and government overthrows and all kinds of death and destruction and hatred all because of where someone was born or how much money they have (or don't have) or whether their families were farmers or bankers.

We studied the Rwandan genocide in school. Over 800,000 deaths and millions of refugees. Neighbors killed neighbors not because of the color of their skin but because of their ancestry – the bridge of their nose, the blood in their veins.

Sometimes I find myself angry at Hailey. With so much death in the world, why did she choose to get in a car with a drunk person? People are struggling to hang on every day and she made such a stupid decision. Why didn't she call her mom or a taxi or walk? When I told my mom that Hailey died she said, "Oh my God," over and over.

The only time I ever hear my mom say the 'G' word is when something terrible happens.

* * *

Dr. Sanderson left her practice. I only saw her once after Hailey died. I guess she tried. She sent a letter to her patients with the names of other doctors in town. Mom said we would "shop around".

XENOPHILIA

NAOMI

"I die, a man fulfilled.
My son shall live to see Israel reborn. I know this.
And what is more, we Jews have avenged our honor as a people."

Leon Uris, *Mila 18*

This is crazy, but I feel that Ruby and I have grown closer since Hailey died. I feel awful even writing this, but no one is going to read it so I suppose I can be brutally honest. I feel as if the weight of tragedy has been lifted a little; as if the burden has been shared. Maybe Hailey's death is a reminder that everyone experiences trauma. Everyone experiences pain. Ruby and I do not have a monopoly on pain.

I feel for Dr. Sanderson. I don't know what it is like to lose a daughter, and I pray I never do. But, I do know what it is like to lose someone; to have that feeling of lead in your stomach. To wake up every day and hope against hope that it has all been a nightmare only to realize that this is the new reality…and will be…forever.

She left her practice, which is good. She needed to. I should have left my job after the shooting. I've stayed too long. I don't want to be there anymore. I'm ready for a new beginning.

Can a tragedy sometimes bring strength and beauty? Like Israel after the Holocaust?

I think so. I am ready for some of the beauty to sneak back in; for some of the strength to return.

* * *

I helped Ruby with her X word: xenophobia — the fear of something strange or foreign. I discovered that the opposite of xenophobia is xenophilia. Xenophilia is affection for strange/foreign objects or people.

I really don't know what to write about that.

Is it enough that I learned a new word?

YIZKOR

RUBY

"Each night, when I go to sleep, I die.
And the next morning, when I wake up, I am reborn."

Mahatma Gandhi

Yizkor means remembrance in Hebrew. Rabbi Nachman of Bratslav said that if a person is able to write a book and does not write it, it is as if one has lost a child. Maybe that's why Dr. Sanderson had me write this journal. I have to admit, I'll miss writing. I am almost at Z and I can think of a million other things to write – so many things I missed. The alphabet is a thin fence.

When I try to remember everything that's happened since the shooting some parts are fuzzy. Was it partly sunny or partly cloudy? Did I like Dr. Sanderson when I first met her? Did Grandma come to visit once a month or once a week? Maybe this means I'm healing. Maybe it means I'm growing. I still don't feel completely "normal". I don't think I ever will. Sometimes I am scared of forgetting. I don't want to forget. Remembrance is strength. The past makes us who we are today, and I don't want to forget the things that have made me who I am.

I want to keep this journal and read it one day when I'm old and I won't even be able to remember writing it. I want to sit on my couch and cover my legs with a blanket and read it all because this journal is my life.

It's sad, and tough, and wonderful.

Maybe other people will read it too. Maybe I'll let my kids read it. Or the person I marry. Maybe my mom will read it. This is who I am. This is my story and it's up to me to remember.

* * *

I'm wearing the gold angel necklace Hailey gave me.

YOU

NAOMI

"I was born with the devil in me.
I could not help the fact that I was a murderer, no more than the poet can
help the inspiration to sing."

Dr. H.H. Holmes, Confession 1896
from Erik Larson's *The Devil in the White City*

I have been thinking a lot about other people. I think one of the reasons is because, during therapy, I had to think mostly about myself. I was asked to revisit my past and to think ahead to my future. In the end, though, we are all one. I know that sounds cheesy. I am not talking about a collective consciousness type of thing. I am just in the midst of realizing that I am a part of humanity. I mean, I have always known that. But, lately, I have come to accept it more. I am part of everyone and everyone is part of me. I have the power to help others just as others have helped me. There are people in this world who need me right now. They could learn from what I have been through. We can all learn from what others have accomplished, have survived, have tended, and have grown.

I suppose I am thinking less about me and more about *you*.

You could be Ruby.

You could be someone I have not yet met.

You could even be me in the future, I suppose.

ZAKA

RUBY

"I slept and I dreamed that life is all joy. I woke and I saw that life is all service. I served and I saw that service is joy."

Kahlil Gibran

In Israel, there is a group of mostly Orthodox Jews who assist ambulance crews, aid in the identification of the victims of terrorism, road accidents and other disasters, and gather body parts and spilled blood for proper burial. They are called ZAKA.

ZAKA stands for *Zihuy Korbanot Ason*. In English, Disaster Victim Identification. I first learned of ZAKA in a Jewish magazine. There was a picture of an ambulance outside a ring of terror – a building in pieces, people bloodied and frozen by the camera in screams and howls.

I wonder how difficult it is to piece bodies back together. Do they match skin color, nail polish, wounds – fitting them together like puzzle pieces?

In Orthodox Judaism, a person's body must be buried intact or at least as close as it can get. The members of ZAKA believe that this is so

123

important, they risk their lives to piece people back together so they can be buried whole.

I know this is a gruesome way to end my journal, but (or is it however) I have been thinking about the ultimate good deed lately. Maimonides, a wise Jewish man, taught that comforting a mourner is better than visiting the sick, because comforting mourners is an act of kindness toward both the living and the dead. If you perform an act of loving kindness for the dead, it is the greatest good deed because the dead cannot repay you.

I will never know Hailey as an adult. Anne Frank never got to be an adult. Neither did the children who perished when the Titanic sunk. My mom's coworkers will never see their children have grandchildren. Dr. Sanderson will never see Hailey's children — what could have been. I guess the thing for me to do is survive, to keep on living. My mom smiles a lot more now. I think her Worry Doctor helps her to keep on living too. Last night she told me that trauma peaks at three years. I don't know if that's true, but she said that it will get easier from this point on. Three years sounds like a long time. To a three-year-old, it's a lifetime. Sometimes I feel like I'm three. I want to throw a tantrum, take naps in my mommy's lap and watch cartoons on Saturday mornings. Mom says that's okay. She says that we are learning to live again post-shooting.

We are like three-year-olds, learning to navigate this new world.

Except, instead of cartoons, Mom asked me to attend synagogue this coming Friday night. She wants to say Kaddish — the Jewish prayer of mourning. She laughed when she asked me to go with her. "The prayer of mourning never mentions death at all," she said. "It's a prayer praising God. Isn't that silly? Someone dies and we praise God."

"Then why do you want to go say it?" I asked.

Mom looked at me and her eyes filled with tears. She wiped them away before they fell. "Because, Ruby, I still can."

There are so many people who can't do what they want to do. They can't get clean drinking water, food to eat, medical care for their children or freedom to practice their religion. Some can't even go to school, or read a book without the threat of death.

We still can. Mom and I.

We are still alive, and for as long as my days last on this earth I want to do what is right, what is good. I won't let the gunman write my future. Maybe that is what this journal has been about all along, writing my own future, on my own terms. It is up to me to remember the past and create the future.

ZERO

NAOMI

"So we beat on, boats against the current,
borne ceaselessly into the past."

F. Scott Fitzgerald, *The Great Gatsby*

One definition for the word zero is a sight setting that enables a firearm to shoot on target. Is that where the term to "set your sights on something" originates? According to the internet, no. But the internet does not know all.

So, let's pretend for a moment that that is exactly where it originates. To set one's sights on something is to decide to achieve something – to set a goal. What if, in order to achieve something, you had to revert to zero? Go back to nothing. Start with a blank slate.

If every time you set a new goal, you had to pick yourself up, wipe yourself off and start anew, would it help you to reach that goal?

And, I don't mean wiping the past from your memory. The past makes you who you are. It is part of you. It builds you up and tears you down and builds you up again. Everyone has a past. If you are here in the present, you have a past. And if you are here in the present, you have a future.

My past is part of me. Every decision I have made is part of who I am, of who I have become. Even though my past is riddled with bullets and lost relationships and sadness, it is also filled with the birth of a precious gem, laughter, and resilience.

In the end, I am lucky. I am grateful.

I said Kaddish again. I glorified a god. Why? Because God is only God because of me. I make God real. I can hold the spark of the divine inside of me and I can breathe light into God.

I have that power.

EPILOGUE

RUBY

It's been 10 years since my mother survived a workplace shooting. Since then there have been hundreds of shootings in America. Many of those were called "mass shootings" by the media. Although there are no set criteria defining mass shootings, they generally refer to crimes involving multiple victims of gun violence. Wouldn't that make every shooting a mass shooting? Even if no one is shot, everyone involved is still a victim of gun violence. Or is a shooting only valid if people are shot? If multiple people are shot, and no one dies is it still considered a mass shooting?

The news defined mom's shooting as a mass shooting. Three people were shot and killed, twelve were shot and survived. That means there were fifteen total, right? What about the children of the women who were murdered?

Are they victims?

What about the families who slept in chairs in hospital rooms while their loved ones recovered?

Are they victims?

What about the people, like mom, who were there but not shot?

Are they victims?

What about me?

When I started seeing Dr. Sanderson it was because my mother survived a shooting and our lives were a mess. I never thought of myself as a victim. I would jump at loud noises, not because I thought they were gun shots, but because I got used to mom screaming every time she heard a balloon pop or a door slam. I would cry a lot, sometimes for no reason. Some nights I couldn't sleep; I was afraid of the nightmares I would have. I never considered myself a victim because I wasn't in the building with the gunman. I wasn't shot. I didn't jump out of my office window.

I realize now that shootings have more victims than bullets. The bullets didn't hit me or my mom but they tore through our lives like the ripples from a bomb.

Are we victims?

Or are we survivors?

When I was in therapy with Dr. Sanderson I swore that when I grew up I would do something that made me happy. I never opened a popcorn stand or an ice cream parlor but I am doing something that makes me happy. I'm writing. I write and illustrate children's books. I guess I have never given up on the innocence of childhood. I still want to be a part of that. To experience that innocence again.

Mom has published three books on the healing power of Haiku. She says that shoving all her thoughts into a 5-7-5 syllable poem helps to make sense of the senseless. It reminds me of when she used to say she shoved all the good and holy in the world into the 'O' in God.

Mom still fights the nightmares, but not as much. She sleeps through most nights and she laughs often.

She still cries every anniversary though. Especially this one, ten years sounds like a long time.

It isn't.

I am happy with my life. Ten years after the worst event of my life and I am happy. It sounds odd. But it is true. Mom is happy too. It feels weird to write, but she is. We both are.

I haven't let Mom read my journal yet. Maybe I will someday.

I am working on my next book. It is called *Ripple*.

I am dedicating it to Hailey Sanderson.

QUESTIONS FOR THOUGHT AND DISCUSSION

The following questions are meant to spur both thought and discussion. They can be used as part of a book club discussion, classroom writing prompts, or individual consideration. Remember to follow each yes or no question with "why/why not", or "explain". The prompt, "tell me more" is always useful. Feel free to add your own questions.

You can share your questions and thoughts with the authors at diameterbullet@gmail.com.

Aftermath

- What do you think Ruby needs help understanding?
- Why do you think Dr. Sanderson uses her own daughter to get closer to Ruby?

Adrenaline

- Why do you think Naomi, Ruby's mom, wanted to write a journal like Ruby's?
- The first time we learn Ruby's name is in the first sentence of Naomi's first entry. Do you find this significant?

Bullets

- Just as we learn Ruby's name from Naomi's entry, we learn Naomi's name from an entry in Ruby's diary. Do you feel there is something meaningful in this?

Balloons

- Have you ever been startled by a balloon popping or something you knew was harmless, but that made you jump? How did you feel? What did you do to calm yourself?

Car Alarms

- Why do you think Ruby used the term "Jewish moms"? Is there a difference between Jewish moms and other moms?

Cortisol

- How do Naomi's journal entries differ from Ruby's in terms of subject and emotion?
- Naomi's doctor tells her she should stop reading so many articles. Do you agree?

December

- Have you ever been scared to tell someone something about yourself, or to be who you really are? How did it feel? What did you do?
- Why do you think Ruby decides not to tell her mom or Dr. Sanderson that Hailey is in her English class?

Dream

- How did this entry differ from Naomi's other entries?
- Is there significance to this dream? Why do you think Naomi chose to write about this dream?

Everything is Messed Up

- What does it mean to be brave?

Evil

- What do you think Naomi means when she uses the term, "the other"?
- How do you feel about Naomi's statement that "we are all, in essence, evil"?

Finality

- Why do you think Naomi chose to share this story with Ruby? Do you feel she should have shared this information?

Forgotten

- If you wore your stories on the outside, what would they say?

God

- Ruby says that she doesn't know what to think or feel about God. She writes a lot about what her mom thought about God, but not what Ruby thinks about God. Why do you think that is?

God

- What do you think Naomi's entry about God says about her feelings toward her religion and her belief in God?

However

- Both Naomi and Ruby have offered definitions to explain a word. Why do you think they choose to define words in their entries?
- Ruby writes that she feels as if they are taking one step forward and three steps back. Have you ever felt like that?

Hate

- Ruby chose not to write about hate. Naomi does write about hate. What do you think this says about their individual healing processes?

Israel

- Ruby admits that she does not know much about Israel, however she writes that the Israeli café experience was "wonderful". Do you think you can appreciate something even if you don't know much about it, or is knowledge about something necessary for appreciation?

I

- Naomi admits that she needs help. Why do you think she would feel guilty asking her real mother for help? Why do you think she would prefer to have a fake mother?

Jewish

- Part of Ruby's identity is being Jewish. What are some parts of your identity? How do they affect who you are in the world?
- Why do you think people wanted to send Naomi Stars of David after the shooting? What do you think it meant for these people who didn't even know Naomi, to send her a Star of David?
- Why do you think Ruby does not want to get together with Hailey and Dr. Sanderson? Have you ever had to do something you didn't want to do?

Jewel

- Naomi named Ruby after a song she heard on the radio. How did you get your name? What does your name mean to you, to your family? Do you think names describe a person?

Knowledge, a posteriori

- How would you answer Ruby's question, "Do you really know anything until you experience it for yourself?"
- Would you have worn the gold angel necklace if you were Ruby?

Kingdom

- Why do you think Naomi chose to stay at her job even after the shooting?

Life

- Ruby wanted her life to be fulfilling. What would fulfill you in life?

Lying

- Why do you think Naomi chose to do something (serve pie on pi day) that she says she hates?
- Do you think Naomi should lie about what she does for a living?

Me

- Ruby wants to be as supple as the reed, but feels as rigid as the cedar. Can you relate to that feeling?

Metaphor

- Have you ever felt like you want someone to *get* you? To really understand what you are saying or feeling? What was that like? What did you do to be understood?
- Naomi writes that what she is really thinking is too scary to say. What do you think Naomi is really thinking? Why is she scared to voice her thoughts?

New

- What do you think of Ruby's new idea of rippling? Can you ripple? What are some ways you can ripple?

Names

- Naomi writes that Leo's social workers "know better". Do you think that is true?
- How do you feel about Naomi's statement that "labels matter"?

Omniscience

- Why do think Naomi described God as a question mark?

Obsessive

- Do you agree that people are unpredictable? Can we predict human behavior? Are there warning signs? If so, what are they?
- Naomi has used the term "point of no return" before. Why do you think she feels (or worries) about reaching this point? What do you think she means by this term?

Postal, as in "Going Postal"

- Ruby wants to 'nip things in the bud', or cut things off before they get too far. What do you think she means by this in relation to preventing shootings? What do you think we can do to prevent such crimes from happening?

PTSD

- Naomi is in group therapy with others who experience PTSD, yet she wants to go home. Why do you think she wants to leave this group? Do you think leaving the group would be helpful or not?

Quixote

- Have you ever felt like you are chasing windmills?
- Why do you think Naomi has two copies of the same book?
- Ruby wonders if her mom would have taken her on a journey like John Steinbeck's trip across America. Why do you think she questions if her mom would have taken her along?

Quiet

- Why do you think it is important for Naomi to hear Ruby?

Revenge

- Have you ever wanted revenge? What did it feel like?
- Why do you think Ruby chooses to let her mom "pretend that she's still 12 years old"?

Raft

- Have you ever imagined something ordinary to be something extraordinary?

Sorry

- Do you think saying sorry helps you heal?

Stethoscope

- Naomi writes that it would be amazing to someday share her story if it could help someone else. How do you think sharing stories can help others? Is it important to share our stories?

Truth and Titanic

- Why do you think so many phrases are gun-related? Can you think of others that Ruby does not list?
- Ruby hopes that if she is ever faced with a time when she has to be true to herself, she is true to others. What do you think she means by that?

Today and Tomorrow

- Naomi knows that tomorrow is not guaranteed for anyone. Why do you think is it hard for her to carry this knowledge and still look forward to a future for her and Ruby?

Ushpizin

- From Ruby's journal entry, how do you think Ruby felt when Hailey died?
- Does Ruby blame anyone for Hailey's death? Should she?

Uncertainty

- Why do you think Naomi feels she needs to be more in touch with Ruby after Hailey died?

Vampires

- Do you agree with Ruby's assessment that people like vampires because they are afraid to die?

Violence

- Why do you think Naomi ends her entry on violence with the words, "I am human"?

Work

- Do you find significance in Dr. Sanderson not mentioning Hailey during her session with Ruby?
- Why do you think Dr. Sanderson chose to go back to work soon after her daughter died?

Worth

- Do you feel that people have become desensitized to shootings? Are they so common now that people don't care as much? What if a tragic event happens elsewhere in the world? Does that make it easier to deal with? To forget about?

Xenophobia

- Why do you think Ruby was angry at Hailey?
- Do you think Ruby was right to be angry?
- Do you think anger can help you heal?

Xenophilia

- What do you think of Naomi's confession that she feels the weight of tragedy has been lifted a little since Hailey died?
- Do you think a tragedy can sometimes bring strength and beauty?
- Naomi does not really write about her X word, xenophilia. Or does she? What do you think?

Yizkor

- What do you think Ruby means by, "The alphabet is a thin fence"?
- Why do you think Ruby chose to wear the gold angel necklace from Hailey?

You

- Naomi is thinking more about others than herself. Do you think this is healthy stage in healing?
- What do you think Naomi means when she writes that *you* could be her in the future?

ZAKA

- Do you feel that choosing ZAKA was a morbid way to end Ruby's journal?
- Do you think Ruby attends services with her mom to say Kaddish?

Zero

- What do you think Naomi means when she says that God is only God because of her?
- Do you think we all hold the spark of the divine inside each of us?

GLOSSARY

Anti-Semitism is hostility, prejudice or discrimination against Jews. A person who holds such positions is called an anti-Semite. Antisemitism is widely considered to be a form of racism.

Bat Mitzvah (for girls) and **Bar Mitzvah** (for boys) are Jewish coming of age rituals. Bar is a Jewish Babylonian Aramaic word literally meaning "son", while bat means "daughter" in Hebrew, and mitzvah means "commandment" or "law". Thus bar mitzvah and bat mitzvah literally translate to "son of commandment" and "daughter of commandment".

A **cantor** is a clergy member who sings and leads prayer in Jewish worship services.

Challah is a braided, leavened egg bread traditionally made to celebrate Shabbat (defined on page 144).

Chanukah is a Jewish festival beginning the 25th day of Kislev, lasting eight days. It commemorates the rededication of the Temple in 165 BCE by the Maccabees after its desecration by the Syrians.

Chesed is a Hebrew word meaning "loving kindness".

Eilat is Israel's southernmost city, a busy port and popular resort at the northern tip of the Red Sea, on the Gulf of Aqaba.

Falafel is a Middle Eastern dish of spiced mashed chickpeas formed into balls or fritters and deep-fried, usually eaten with or in pita bread.

Genocide is the intentional action to systematically eliminate an ethnic, national, racial, or religious group. The word is a combination of "genos" (race, people) and "cide" (to kill). The United Nations Genocide Convention defines it as "acts committed with intent to destroy, in whole or in part, a national, ethnical, racial or religious group".

Haifa is the third-largest city in Israel and a major seaport located on Israel's Mediterranean coastline in the Bay of Haifa.

Hebrew is the language used to record the Torah and many Jewish prayers and texts. It is also the dominant language of Israel.

The **Holocaust**, also known as the Shoah, was a genocide in which Adolf Hitler's Nazi Germany and its collaborators killed about six million Jews. The victims included 1.5 million children and represented about two-thirds of the nine million Jews who had resided in Europe. Some definitions of the Holocaust include the additional five million non-Jewish victims of Nazi mass murders, bringing the total to about 11 million. Killings took place throughout Nazi Germany and German-occupied territories.

Hummus is a thick paste or spread traditionally made from ground chickpeas and sesame seeds, olive oil, lemon, and garlic, made originally in the Middle East.

Israel is a country in the Middle East, on the southeastern shore of the Mediterranean Sea and the northern shore of the Red Sea. It has land borders with Lebanon to the north, Syria to the northeast, Jordan on the east, the Palestinian territories of the West Bank and Gaza Strip to the east and west, respectively, and Egypt to the southwest. It contains geographically diverse features within its relatively small area.

Maimonides was a Sephardic Jewish philosopher, astronomer, physician, and one of the most influential Torah scholars of the Middle Ages.

A **menorah** is a candelabrum used in Jewish worship, especially one with eight branches and a central socket used at Chanukah.

Morah means teacher in Hebrew. *Morah* is feminine and *Moreh* is masculine.

Mourner's Kaddish is a prayer said by Jews in mourning.

Orthodox Judaism is the branch of Judaism that has the strictest adherence to traditional Jewish practices and beliefs.

Passover (or *Pesach* in Hebrew) is a spring festival that commemorates the liberation of Jews from Egyptian slavery.

Post-Traumatic Stress Disorder or **PTSD** is a mental health condition that is triggered by a terrifying event — either experiencing it or witnessing it. Symptoms may include flashbacks, nightmares and severe anxiety, as well as uncontrollable thoughts about the event.

A **rabbi** is a Jewish scholar or teacher, especially one who studies or teaches Jewish law; also a person appointed as a Jewish religious leader.

The **Red Balloon** is a 1956 French fantasy comedy-drama featurette written, produced, and directed by Albert Lamorisse. The tale follows the adventures of a young boy who one day finds a sentient, mute, red balloon.

Shabbat (Sabbath) is observed by Jews from sundown on Friday to sundown Saturday. It is a time of rest and reflection, celebrated with the lighting of candles, wine, challah and songs/prayers.

A **Star of David** is a six-pointed figure consisting of two interlaced equilateral triangles, used as a Jewish and Israeli symbol.

A **sukkah** (Hebrew), often translated as "booth", is a temporary hut constructed for use during the week-long Jewish festival of Sukkot. It is topped with branches and often decorated with autumnal, harvest, or Judaic themes.

Sukkot (Hebrew) literally means Feast of Booths and is commonly translated in English as Feast of Tabernacles. It is a biblical Jewish holiday celebrated on the 15th day of the month of Tishrei (varies from late September to late October). During the existence of the Jerusalem Temple it was one of the Three Pilgrimage Festivals on which the Israelites were commanded to perform a pilgrimage to the Temple.

A **synagogue** is a place for a Jewish congregation to gather for religious worship and learning.

Tahini is a Middle Eastern paste or sauce made from ground sesame seeds.

Tel Aviv is a major city in Israel, the second-most populous city administered by the Israeli government after Jerusalem. It is situated on the Mediterranean coastline in central-west Israel.

Torah is the law upon which Judaism is founded. Torah is also a scroll containing the first five books of the Bible.

PEOPLE AND WORKS QUOTED

IN ALPHABETICAL ORDER (BY LAST NAME)

Mitchell David "Mitch" Albom was born May 23, 1958 and is an American best-selling author, journalist, screenwriter, dramatist, radio and television broadcaster, and musician. He is best known for the inspirational stories and themes that weave through his books, plays, and films. His book, *Tuesdays with Morrie*, was published in 1997 and is a memoir which topped the New York Times Non-Fiction Bestsellers of 2000.

Durante degli Alighieri simply called Dante (c. 1265 – 1321), was a major Italian poet of the late Middle Ages. His *Divine Comedy*, originally called *Comedìa* is widely considered the greatest literary work composed in the Italian language and a masterpiece of world literature.

Yehuda Amichai was born May 3, 1924 and died September 22, 2000. He was an Israeli poet. Amichai is considered by many, both in Israel and internationally, as Israel's greatest modern poet. He was also one of the first to write in colloquial Hebrew. Amichai's poem, *The Diameter of the Bomb*, was the inspiration for the title of this book.

Maya Angelou was born Marguerite Annie Johnson April 4, 1928 and died May 28, 2014. She was an American author, poet, and civil rights activist. Her first autobiography, *I Know Why the Caged Bird Sings* (1969), tells of her life up to age 17 and brought her international recognition and acclaim.

Christine Arnothy was 15 years old when she lived through the events told about in her book, *I Am Fifteen – and I Don't Want to Die*. Her book is the true story of teenage heartbreak and heroism during World War II. Arnothy left Hungary in 1948 and was working in a bookstore in Belgium when she began writing the book from the diaries that she had kept during the siege of Budapest. *I Am Fifteen – and I Don't Want to Die* won the Prix de Verites (French prize for nonfiction) the year it was published (1956).

Margaret Atwood was born November 18, 1939. She is a Canadian poet, novelist, literary critic, essayist, and environmental activist. Her books have received critical acclaim in the United States, Europe, and her native Canada, and she has received numerous literary awards, including the Booker Prize, the Arthur C. Clarke Award, and the Governor General's Award, twice.

The **Babylonian Talmud** was compiled about the year 500, although it continued to be edited later. The older compilation is called the Jerusalem Talmud or the *Talmud Yerushalmi*. It was compiled in the 4th century CE in Galilee. The word "Talmud", when used without qualification, usually refers to the Babylonian Talmud.

Stanley W. Beesley is the author of *Vietnam: The Heartland Remembers*. This oral history offers the voices of thirty-three Oklahomans. In the ranks of the compilation are reluctant warriors, gung ho marines, skeptics, embittered former patriots, and humanists. These men and women recount their experiences not as heroes but as ordinary people thrust by politics and fate into the uncommon circumstances of the Vietnam War.

Elise Blackwell was born July 8, 1964 in Austin, Texas. She was primarily raised in southern Louisiana. She studied creative writing at Louisiana State University before entering the MFA Program of the University of California, Irvine. Her novel, *Hunger*, was published in 2003 is an account of the 900-day long siege of Leningrad which began in the fall of 1941. As the first "hunger winter" sets in, the scientists at the Institute of Plant Industry pledge to protect their collection of rare seeds, painstakingly gathered from all over the world, no matter the human cost.

Judy Blume wan born February 12, 1938. She is an American writer known for children's and young adult (YA) fiction. Blume's novel, *In the Unlikely Event* tells the story of a time when a succession of airplanes fell from the sky, leaving a community reeling. This story is based on actual events that Blume experienced in the early 1950s, when airline travel was new and exciting and everyone dreamed of going somewhere.

William Cullen Bryant was born November 3, 1794 and died June 12, 1878. He was an American romantic poet, journalist, and long-time editor of the *New York Evening Post*. "Thanatopsis" is Bryant's most famous poem, which Bryant may have been working on as early as 1811.

Edmund Burke was born January 12, 1729 and died July 9, 1797. Burke was an Irish statesman born in Dublin, as well as an author, orator, political theorist and philosopher who, after moving to London, served as a Member of Parliament for many years in the House of Commons with the Whig Party.

Albert Camus was born November 7, 1913 and died January 4, 1960. He was a French philosopher, author, and journalist. His views contributed to the rise of the philosophy known as absurdism. He wrote in his essay *The Rebel* that his whole life was devoted to opposing the philosophy of nihilism while still delving deeply into individual freedom. He won the Nobel Prize in Literature in 1957.

Miguel de Cervantes is thought to have been born September 29, 1547 and died April 22, 1616. He is widely regarded as the greatest writer in the Spanish language. His major work, *Don Quixote*, considered to be the first modern European novel, is a classic of Western literature, and is regarded amongst the best works of fiction ever written.

Breena Clarke, grew up in Washington D.C., and was educated at Webster College and Howard University. Her 1999 novel, *River, Cross my Heart*, focuses on the Georgetown neighborhood of Washington D.C., circa 1926 as the community tries to grapple with the tragic death of a young girl. Clarke survived the death of her only child and writes with depth and clarity about grief.

Samuel Langhorne Clemens, better known by his pen name **Mark Twain**, was born November 30, 1835 and died April 21, 1910. He was an American author and humorist. He wrote *The Adventures of Tom Sawyer* (1876) and its sequel, *Adventures of Huckleberry Finn* (1885), the latter often called "The Great American Novel".

Sonali Deraniyagala was born in 1964 in Colombo, Sri Lanka. She studied economics at Cambridge University and has a doctorate from the University of Oxford. In December 2004 she was on vacation at Sri Lanka's Yala National Park. Deraniyagala lost her two sons, her husband, and her parents in the Indian Ocean tsunami. The tsunami carried her two miles inland and she was able to survive by clinging to a tree branch. Her 2013 memoir, *Wave*, recounts her experiences in the tsunami and the progression of her grief.

Walter Elias "Walt" Disney was born December 5, 1901 and died December 15, 1966. He was an American entrepreneur, animator, voice actor, and film producer. He was a prominent figure within the American animation industry and throughout the world, and is regarded as a cultural icon, known for his influence and contributions to entertainment during the 20th century. As a Hollywood business mogul, he and his brother Roy O. Disney co-founded The Walt Disney Company.

Ecclesiastes is one of 24 books of the *Tanakh* or Hebrew Bible, where it is classified as one of the *Ketuvim*, or "Writings". It is among the canonical Wisdom Books in the Old Testament of most denominations of Christianity.

Albert Einstein was born March 14, 1879 and died April 18 1955. He was a German-born theoretical physicist. He developed the general theory of relativity, one of the two pillars of modern physics (alongside quantum mechanics). Einstein is best known in popular culture for his mass-energy equivalence formula $E = mc^2$ (which has been dubbed "the world's most famous equation"). He received the 1921 Nobel Prize in Physics for his "services to theoretical physics", in particular his discovery of the law of the photoelectric effect, a pivotal step in the evolution of quantum theory.

Ralph Waldo Emerson was born May 25, 1803 and died April 27, 1882. He was an American essayist, lecturer, and poet who led the Transcendentalist movement of the mid-19th century. He was seen as a champion of individualism and a prescient critic of the countervailing pressures of society, and he disseminated his thoughts through dozens of published essays and more than 1,500 public lectures across the United States.

Francis Scott Key Fitzgerald was born September 24, 1896 and died December 21, 1940. He was an American novelist and short story writer during the Jazz Age. Fitzgerald is considered a member of the "Lost Generation" of the 1920s. He finished four novels: *This Side of Paradise, The Beautiful and Damned, The Great Gatsby* (his best known), and *Tender Is the Night*. A fifth, unfinished novel, *The Love of the Last Tycoon*, was published posthumously.

Annelies (Anne) Marie Frank was born June 12, 1929 and died in February or March of 1945. Anne Frank was a German-born diarist and writer. She is one of the most discussed Jewish victims of the Holocaust. Her diary, *The Diary of a Young Girl*, which documents her life in hiding during the German occupation of the Netherlands in World War II, is one of the world's most widely known books and has been the basis for several plays and films.

Mahatma Gandhi (Mohandas Karamchand Gandhi) was born October 2, 1869 and died January 30, 1948. Gandhi was the preeminent leader of the Indian independence movement in British-ruled India. Employing nonviolent civil disobedience, Gandhi led India to independence and inspired movements for civil rights and freedom across the world. The honorific Mahatma is Sanskrit for "high-souled" or "venerable" and was first applied to him in 1914 in South Africa.

Khalil Gibran was born January 6 1883 and died April 10, 1931. He was a Lebanese-American artist, poet, and writer of the New York Pen League. He is chiefly known in the English-speaking world for his 1923 book *The Prophet*, an early example of inspirational fiction including a series of philosophical essays written in poetic English prose.

Elizabeth Gilbert was born in Waterbury, Connecticut on July 18, 1969. She is an American author, essayist, short story writer, biographer, novelist and memoirist. She is best known for her 2006 memoir, *Eat, Pray, Love.*

Thom Gunn was born in Gravesend, England. Both of his parents were journalists. They divorced when he was 10 years old. When he was a teenager his mother killed herself. It was she who had sparked in him a love of reading.

Ernest Miller Hemingway was born July 21, 1899 and died July 2, 1961. Hemingway was an American novelist, short story writer, and journalist. His economical and understated style had a strong influence on 20th-century fiction, while his life of adventure and his public image influenced later generations. Hemingway produced most of his work between the mid-1920s and the mid-1950s, and won the Nobel Prize in Literature in 1954.

Thor Heyerdahl was born October 6, 1914 and died April 18, 2002. He was a Norwegian adventurer and ethnographer with a background in zoology, botany, and geography. He became notable for his Kon-Tiki expedition in 1947, in which he sailed 8,000 km (5,000 mi) across the Pacific Ocean in a hand-built raft from South America to the Tuamotu Islands. The expedition was designed to demonstrate that ancient people could have made long sea voyages, creating contacts between separate cultures.

James Mercer Langston Hughes was born in Joplin, Missouri February 1, 1902 and died May 22, 1967. Hughes was an American poet, social activist, novelist, playwright, and columnist. He was one of the earliest innovators of the literary art form, jazz poetry. Hughes is best known as a leader of the Harlem Renaissance.

Stephen King was born September 21, 1947. King is an American author of contemporary horror, supernatural fiction, suspense, science fiction, and fantasy. His books have sold more than 350 million copies. His horror novel, *It*, was published in 1986 and follows seven children as they are terrorized by a being, which exploits the fears and phobias of its victims in order to disguise itself. The novel is told through narratives alternating between two time periods.

Erik Larson was born January 3, 1954. He is an American journalist and author of nonfiction books. He has written a number of bestsellers such as *The Devil in the White City* (2003), about the 1893 World's Columbian Exposition in Chicago and a series of murders by H. H. Holmes that were committed in the city around the time of the Fair. *The Devil in the White City* also won the 2004 Edgar Award in the Best Fact Crime category. The authors attribute the quote at the beginning of Naomi's chapter titled YOU to Larson purposely – so as not to give a serial killer additional purchase.

Mary Lawson was born in 1946 in southwestern Ontario, Canada and is a distant relative of L. M. Montgomery, author of *Anne of Green Gables*. Lawson spent her summers in the north, and the landscape inspired her to use northern Ontario as her settings for both of her novels. *The Other Side of the Bridge* is her second novel. It became a bestseller in Canada, and was longlisted for The Booker Prize.

Margaret Munnerlyn Mitchell was born November 8, 1900 and died August 16, 1949. Mitchell was an American author and journalist. One novel by Mitchell was published during her lifetime, the American Civil War-era novel, *Gone with the Wind*, for which she won the National Book Award for Most Distinguished Novel of 1936 and the Pulitzer Prize for Fiction in 1937.

Mourner's Kaddish is an ancient Jewish liturgical prayer largely written in Aramaic and used in various forms to separate sections of the liturgy. Mourners have the right to recite some of these in public prayer during the year after, and on the anniversary of, a death.

Scott O'Dell was born May 23, 1898 and died October 15, 1989. He was an American author of 26 novels for young people, along with three novels for adults and four nonfiction books. O'Dell's best known work is the historical novel, *Island of the Blue Dolphins* (1960), which won the 1961 Newbery Medal.

Ayn Rand was a Russian-born American novelist, philosopher, playwright, and screenwriter. She is known for her two best-selling novels, *The Fountainhead* and *Atlas Shrugged*, and for developing a philosophical system she called Objectivism. Her dystopian fiction novella, *Anthem,* takes place at some unspecified future date when mankind has entered another dark age. Technological advancement is now carefully planned and the concept of individuality has been eliminated.

Fred Rogers is most commonly known as Mr. Rogers. He was born March 20, 1928 and died February 27, 2003. Rogers was most famous for creating, hosting, and composing the theme music for the educational preschool television show Mister Rogers' Neighborhood (1968–2001). Rogers received the Presidential Medal of Freedom, a Peabody Award, and was inducted into the Television Hall of Fame.

Anna Eleanor Roosevelt was born October 11, 1884 and died November 7, 1962. She was an American politician, diplomat, and activist. She was First Lady of the United States from March 1933 to April 1945 during her husband President Franklin D. Roosevelt's four terms in office, and served as United States Delegate to the United Nations General Assembly from 1945 to 1952. President Harry S. Truman later called her the "First Lady of the World" in tribute to her human rights achievements.

Bertrand Arthur William Russell, 3rd Earl Russell, was born May 18, 1872 and died February 2, 1970. He was a British philosopher, logician, mathematician, historian, writer, social critic, political activist and Nobel laureate. He was born in Monmouthshire into one of the most prominent aristocratic families in the United Kingdom.

Thomas J. Shuell holds a Ph.D. in Educational Psychology from the University of California, Berkeley, (1967) and a B.S., in General Science with a Mathematics minor from Oregon State University (1960). His research interests include: learning and cognition, teaching methods and theories, and instructional technology and its applications in schools and universities.

John Ernst Steinbeck, Jr. was born February 27, 1902 and died December 20, 1968. He was an American author of twenty-seven books, including sixteen novels, six non-fiction books, and five collections of short stories. He is widely known for the comic novels *Tortilla Flat* (1935) and *Cannery Row* (1945), the multi-generation epic *East of Eden* (1952), and the novellas

Of Mice and Men (1937) and *The Red Pony* (1937). The Pulitzer Prize-winning *The Grapes of Wrath* (1939), is considered Steinbeck's masterpiece. *Travels with Charley: In Search of America* is a travelogue depicting a 1960 road trip around the United States made by Steinbeck, in the company of his standard poodle, Charley.

Maria Wisława Anna Szymborska was born July 2, 1923 and died February 1, 2012. She was a Polish poet, essayist, translator and recipient of the 1996 Nobel Prize in Literature. She is described as a "Mozart of Poetry". Her poem, *The One Twenty Pub*, is also known as *The Terrorist, He Watches*.

Leon Marcus Uris was born August 3, 1924 and died June 21, 2003. He was an American author, known for his historical fiction. Uris was born in Baltimore, Maryland, the son of Jewish American parents. His book, *Mila 18*, is about the Warsaw ghetto uprising.

Andy Weir was hired as a programmer for a national laboratory when he was just fifteen years old. He worked as a software engineer ever since. Weir is a devoted hobbyist of subjects such as relativistic physics, orbital mechanics, and the history of manned space flight. His novel, *The Martian*, was published in 2011.

Eliezer "Elie" Wiesel was born September 30, 1928. He is a Romanian-born Jewish writer, professor, political activist, and Nobel Laureate. He is the author of 57 books, including *Night*, a work based on his experiences as a prisoner in the Auschwitz, Buna, and Buchenwald concentration camps.

ACKOWLEDGMENTS

The authors wish to thank many individuals and entities who helped in the creation of this book, but especially the following:

Sandra Kaiser, for bringing shoes and being there.
Max Kaiser and Ian Kaiser, for being extraordinary brothers and sons.
Toree Goldstein, for never giving up on us.
Rabbi Michael Adam Latz, for not being afraid to say what needed to be said.

The leaders and congregations of:
Temple B'nai Torah, Bellevue, WA
Kol HaNeshamah, Seattle, WA
Congregation Albert, Albuquerque, NM
Temple Beit HaYam, Stuart, FL

Our First Reader, Jayme Kostandinu
Our Editor, Valerie Gow

Thank you to all whose stories inspired us and nourished our souls along the path of writing this book.

To dear friends who have lost their children too early (you know who you are).

And especially, to those who experienced July 28, 2006 in all its many ripples.